A JACK RYDER NOVEL

HIT THE ROAD JACK

THE MILLION-COPY BESTSELLING WRITER

WILLOW ROSE

Cover design by Jan Sigetty Boeje
https://www.buoy-media.com

Special thanks to my editor Janell Parque
http://janellparque.blogspot.com/

**To be the first to hear about new releases and bargains from
Willow Rose. Sign up to be on the VIP list below.**
I promise not to share your email with anyone else, and I
won't clutter your inbox.

http://readerlinks.com/l/415254

Tired of too many emails? Text the word: "willowrose" to
31996 to sign up to Willow's VIP text List to get a text alert
with news about New Releases, Giveaways, Bargains and
Free books from Willow.

This could be Heaven or this could be Hell

~ **Eagles, Hotel California 1977**

Prologue

DON'T COME BACK NO MORE

May 2012

She has no idea who she is or where she is and cares to know neither. For some time, for what seems like forever, she has been in this daze. This haze, in complete darkness with nothing but the sounds. Sounds coming from outside her body, from outside her head. Sometimes, the sounds fade and there is only the darkness.

As time passes, she becomes aware that there are two realities. The one in her mind, filled with darkness and pain and then the one outside of her, where something or someone else is living, acting, smelling and…singing.

Yes, that's it. Someone is singing. Does she know the song?

…*What you say?*

The darkness is soon replaced by light. Still, her eyes are too heavy to open. Her consciousness returns slowly. Enough to start asking questions. Where is she? How did she end up here? A series of pictures of her at home come to her mind. She is waiting. What is she waiting for?

…*I guess if you said so.*

Him. She is waiting for him. She is checking her hair in the mirror every five minutes or so. Then correcting the make-up, looking at the clock again. Where is he? She looks out through the window and at the street and the many staring neighboring windows. A feeling of guilt hits her. Somehow, it seems wrong for this kind of thing to take place in broad daylight.

...*That's right!*

A car drives up. The anticipation. The butterflies in her stomach. The sound of the doorbell. She is straightening her dress and taking a last glance in the mirror. The next second, she is in his embrace. He is holding her so tight she closes her eyes and breathes him in until his lips cover hers and she swims away.

...*Whoa, Woman, oh woman, don't treat me so mean.*

His breath is pumping against her skin. She feels his hands on her breasts, under her skirt, coming closer, while he presses her up against the wall. She feels him in her hand. He is hard now, moaning in her ear.

"Where's your husband?" he whispers.

"Work," she moans back, feeling self-conscious. Why did he have to bring up her husband? The guilt is killing her. "The kids are in school."

"Good," he moans. "No one can ever know. Remember that. No one."

...*You're the meanest old woman that I've ever seen.*

He pushes himself inside of her and pumps. She lets herself get into the moment, but as soon as it is over, she finds herself regretting it...while he zips up the pants of his suit and kisses her gently on the lips, whispering, *same time next week*? She regrets having started it all. They are both married with children, and this is only an affair. Could never be anything else, even if she dreamt about it. The sex is great, but she wants more than just seeing him on her lunch break. But she can never tell him. She can never explain to him how much she hates this awkward moment that follows the sex.

"They're expecting me at the office...I have a meeting," he says, and puts his tie back on. "I'd better..."

...*Hit the road, Jack!*

She finally opens her eyes with a loud gasp. The bright light hurts her. Water is being splashed in her face. She can't breathe. The bathtub is slippery when she tries to get up. Her eyes lock with another set of eyes. The eyes of a man. He is staring at her with a twisted smile. She gasps again, suddenly remembering those dark chili eyes.

"*I guess if you said so...I'd have to pack my things and go,*" he sings.

"You," she gasps. Breathing is hard for her. She feels like she is still choking. She is hyperventilating. Panicking.

The man smiles. On his neck crawls a snake. How does that old saying go again? *Red, black, yellow kills a fellow?* This one is all of that, all those colors. It stares at her while moving its tongue back and forth. The man is holding a washcloth in his hand. She looks down at her naked body. The smell of chlorine is strong and makes her eyes water.

"You tried to kill me," she says, while panting with anxiety.

I have to get home. Help me. I have to get home to my children! Oh, God. I can hear their voices! Am I going mad? I think I can hear them!

"I guess I didn't do a very good job, then," he answers. His chillingly calm voice is piercing through every bone in her body.

"I'll try again. *That's right!*"

2

May 2012

S he had never been more beautiful than in this exact moment. No woman ever had. So fragile, her skin so pale it almost looked bluish. The man who called himself the Snakecharmer stared at her body. It was still in the bathtub. He was still panting from the exertion, his hands shaking and hurting from strangling the girl. He felt so aroused in this moment, staring at the dead body. It was the most fascinating thing in the world. How the body simply ceased to function. And almost as fascinating was what followed next. The human decaying process. It wasn't something new. Fascination with death had occurred all throughout human history, characterized by obsessions with death and all things related to death. The Egyptians mummified their dead. He had always wished he could do the same. Keep his dead forever and ever. He remembered as a child how he would sometimes lie down in front of the mirror and try to lie completely still and look at himself, imagining he was looking at a dead body. He would capture cats and kill them and keep them in his room, just to watch what would happen to them. He wanted so badly to stop the decaying process, he wanted them to remain the same always and never leave.

The Snakecharmer stared at the girl with fascination in his

eyes. He caught his breath and calmed down again. He still felt the adrenalin rushing through his veins while he finished washing the girl. He washed away all the dirt, all the smells on her body. He reached down and cleaned her thoroughly between her legs. Scrubbed her to make sure he got all the dirt away, all the filth and impurities.

Then, he dried her with a towel before he pulled her onto the bathroom floor. His companions, his two pet Coral snakes, were sliding across her dead body. He grabbed one and let it slide across his arm while petting it. Then he knelt next to the girl and stroked her gently across her hair, making sure it wasn't in her face. Her blue eyes stared into the ceiling.

"Now, you'll never leave," he whispered.

With his cellphone, he took a picture of her naked body. That was his mummification. His way to always cherish the moment. To always remember. He never wanted to forget how beautiful she was.

He dried her with a towel. He brushed her brown hair with gentle strokes. He took yet another picture before he lifted her up and carried her into the bedroom, where he placed her in a chair, then sat in front of her and placed his head in her lap.

They would stay like this until she started to smell.

Part One

I GUESS IF YOU SAY SO

3

January 2015

He took the dog out in the yard and shut the door carefully behind him, making sure he didn't make a sound to wake up his sleeping parents. It was Monday, but they had been very loud last night. The kitchen counter was still covered with empty bottles.

At first, Ben had waited patiently in the living room, watching a couple of shows on TV, waiting for his parents to wake up. When the clock passed nine, he knew he wouldn't make it to school that day either, and that was too bad because they had a fieldtrip to the zoo today and Ben had been looking forward to it. When they still hadn't shown up at ten o'clock, he decided the dog had to go out. The old Labrador kept sitting by the door and scraping on it. It had to go.

So, Ben took Bobby out in the backyard. He had to go with him. The yard ended at the canal, and Bobby had more than once jumped into the water. Ben had to keep an eye on him to make sure he didn't do it again. It had been such a mess last time, since the dog couldn't climb back up over the seawall on his own, so Ben's dad had to jump into the blurry water and carry the dog out.

The dog quickly gave in to nature and did his business.

Ben had a plastic bag that he picked it up with and threw it in the trash can behind the house.

It was a beautiful day out. One of those clear days with a blue sky and not a cloud anywhere on the horizon. The wind was blowing out of the north and had been for two days, making the air drier. For once, Ben's shirt didn't stick to his body.

He threw the ball a few times for the dog to get some exercise. Ben could smell the ocean, even though he lived on the back side of the barrier island. When it was quiet, he could even hear it too. The waves had to be good. If he wasn't too sick from drinking last night, his dad might take him surfing.

Ben really hoped he would.

It had been months since his dad last took him to the beach. He never seemed to have time anymore. Sometimes, Ben would take his bike and ride down there by himself, but it was never as much fun as when the entire family went. They never seemed to do much together anymore. Ben wondered if it had anything to do with what happened to his baby sister a year ago. He never understood exactly what had happened. He just knew she didn't wake up one morning when their mother went to pick her up from her crib. Then his parents cried and cried for days and they had held a big funeral. But the crying hadn't stopped for a long time. Not until it was replaced with a lot of sleeping and his parents staying up all night, and all the empty bottles that Ben often cleaned up from the kitchen and put in the recycling bin.

Bobby brought back the ball and placed it at Ben's feet. He picked it up and threw it again. It landed close to the seawall. Luckily, it didn't fall in. Bobby ran to get it, then placed it at Ben's feet again, looking at him expectantly.

"Really? One more time, then we're done," he said, thinking he'd better get back inside and start cleaning up. He picked up the ball and threw it. The dog stormed after it again and disappeared for a second down the hill leading to the canal. Ben couldn't see him.

"Bobby?" he yelled. "Come on, boy. We need to get back inside."

He stared in the direction of the canal. He couldn't see the bottom of the yard. He had no idea if Bobby had jumped in the water again. His heart started to pound. He would have to wake up his dad if he did. He was the only one who could get Bobby out of the water.

Ben stood frozen for a few seconds until he heard the sound of Bobby's collar, and a second later spotted his black dog running towards him with his tongue hanging out of his mouth.

"Bobby!" Ben said. He bent down and petted his dog and best friend. "You scared me, buddy. You forgot the ball. Well, we'll have to get that later. Now, let's go back inside and see if Mom and Dad are awake."

Ben grabbed the handle and opened the door. He let Bobby go in first.

"Mom?" he called.

But there was no answer. They were probably still asleep. Ben found some dog food in the cabinet and pulled the bag out. He spilled on the floor when he filled Bobby's tray. He had no idea how much the dog needed, so he made sure to give him enough, and poured till the bowl overflowed. Ben found a garbage bag under the sink and had removed some of the bottles, when Bobby suddenly started growling. The dog ran to the bottom of the stairs and barked. Ben found this to be strange. It was very unlike Bobby to act this way.

"What's the matter, boy? Are Mom and Dad awake?"

The dog kept barking and growling.

"Stop it!" Ben yelled, knowing how much his dad hated it when Bobby barked. "Bad dog."

But Bobby didn't stop. He moved closer and closer to the stairs and kept barking until the dog finally ran up the stairs.

"No! Bobby!" Ben yelled. "Come back down here!"

Ben stared up the stairs after the dog, wondering if he dared to go up there. His dad always got so mad if he went upstairs when they were sleeping. He wasn't allowed up there until they got out of bed. But, if he found Bobby up there, his dad would get really mad. Probably talk about getting rid of him again.

He's my best friend. Don't take my friend away.

"Bobby," he whispered. "Come back down here."

Ben's heart was racing in his chest. There wasn't a sound coming from upstairs. Ben held his breath, not knowing what to do. The last thing he wanted on a day like today was to make his dad angry. He expected his dad to start yelling any second now.

Oh no, what if he jumps into their bed? Dad is going to get so mad. He's gonna get real mad at Bobby.

"Bobby?" Ben whispered a little louder.

There was movement on the stairs, the black lab peeked his head out, then ran down the stairs.

"There you are," Ben said with relief. Bobby ran past him and sprang up on the couch.

"What do you have in your mouth? Not one of mom's shoes again."

It didn't look like it was big enough to be a shoe. Ben walked closer, thinking if it was a pair of Mommy's panties again, then the dog was dead. He reached down and grabbed the dog's mouth, then opened it and pulled out whatever it was. He looked down with a small shriek at what had come out of the dog's mouth. He felt nauseated, like the time when he had the stomach-bug and spent the entire night in the bathroom. Only this was worse.

It's a finger. A finger wearing Mommy's ring!

4

January 2015

"Hit the road, Jack, and don't you come back no more no more no more."

The children's voices were screaming more than singing on the bus. I preferred *Wheels on the Bus,* but the kids thought it was oh so fun, since my name was Jack and I was actually driving the bus. I had volunteered to drive them to the Brevard Zoo for their field trip today. Two of the children, the pretty blonde twins in the back named Abigail and Austin, were mine. A boy and a girl. Just started Kindergarten six months ago. I could hardly believe how fast time passed. Everybody told me it would, but still. It was hard to believe.

I was thirty-five and a single dad of three children. My wife, Arianna, ran out on us four years ago…when the twins were almost two years old. It was too much, she told me. She couldn't cope with the children or me. She especially had a hard time taking care of Emily. Emily was my ex-partner's daughter. My ex-partner, Lisa, was shot on duty ten years ago during a chase in downtown Miami. The shooter was never captured, and it haunted me daily. I took Emily in after her mother died. What else could I have done? I felt guilty for what had happened to her mother. I was supposed to have protected my partner. Plus, the girl didn't know her father. Lisa never told anyone who he was; she didn't have any of her parents or siblings left, except for a homeless brother who was in no condition to take care of a child. So, I got custody and decided to give Emily the best life I could. She was six when I took her in, sixteen now, and at an age where it was hard for anyone to love you, besides your mom and dad. I tried hard to be both for her. Not always with much success. The fact was, I had no idea what it was like to be a black teenage girl.

Personally, I believed Arianna had depression after the birth of the twins, but she never let me close enough to talk about it. She cried for months after the twins were born, then one day out of the blue, she told me she had to go. That she couldn't stay or it would end up killing her. I cried and begged her to stay, but there was nothing I could do. She had made up her mind. She was going back upstate, and that was all I needed to know. I shouldn't look for her, she said.

"Are you coming back?" I asked, my voice breaking. I couldn't believe anyone would leave her own children.

"I don't know, Jack."

"But…The children? They need you? They need their mother?"

"I can't be the mother you want me to be, Jack. I'm just not cut out for it. I'm sorry."

Then she left. Just like that. I had no idea how to explain it to the kids, but somehow I did. As soon as they started asking questions, I told them their mother had left and that I believed she was coming back one day. Some, maybe a lot of people, including my mother, might have told me it was insane to tell them that she might be coming back, but that's what I did. I couldn't bear the thought of them growing up with the knowledge that their own mother didn't want them. I couldn't bear for Emily to know that she was part of the reason why Arianna had left us, left the twins motherless. I just couldn't. I had to leave them with some sort of hope. And maybe I needed to believe it too. I needed to believe that she hadn't just abandoned us…that she had some stuff she needed to work out and soon she would be back. At least for the twins. They needed their mother and asked for her often. It was getting harder and harder for me to believe she was coming back for them. But I still said she would.

And there they were.

On the back seat of the bus, singing along with their class-mates, happier than most of them. Mother or no mother, I had provided a good life for them in our little town of Cocoa Beach. As a detective working for the Brevard County Sher-iff's Office, working their homicide unit, I had lots of spare time and they had their grandparents close by. They received all the love in the world from me and their grandparents, who loved them to death (and let them get away with just about anything).

Some might think they were spoiled brats, but to me they were the love of my life, the light, the...the...

What the heck were they doing in the back?

I hit the brakes a little too hard at the red light. All the kids on the bus fell forwards. The teacher, Mrs. Allen, whined and held on to her purse.

"Abigail and Austin!" I thundered through the bus. "Stop that right now!"

The twins grinned and looked at one another, then continued to smear chocolate on each other's faces. Chocolate from those small boxes with Nutella and sticks you dipped in it. Boxes their grandmother had given them for snack, even though I told her it had to be healthy.

"Now!" I yelled.

"Sorry, Dad," they yelled in unison.

"Well...wipe that off or..."

I never made it any further before the phone in my pocket vibrated. I pulled it out and started driving again as the light turned green.

"Ryder. We need you. I spoke with Ron and he told me you would be assisting us. We desperately need your help."

It was the head of the Cocoa Beach Police Department. Weasel, we called her. I didn't know why. Maybe it had to do with the fact that her name was Weslie Seal. Maybe it was just because she kind of looked like a weasel because her body was long and slender, but her legs very short. Ron Harper was the county sheriff and my boss.

"Yes? When?"

"Now."

"But…I'm…"

"This is big. We need you now."

"If you say so. I'll get there as fast as I can," I said, and turned off towards the entrance to the zoo. The kids all screamed with joy when they saw the sign. Mrs. Allen shushed them.

"What, are you running a day-care now? Not that I have the time to care. Everything is upside down around here. We have a dead body. I'll text you the address. Meet you there."

5

April 1984

Annie was getting ready. She was putting on make-up with her room-mate Julia, while listening to Michael Jackson's *Thriller* and singing into their hairbrushes. They were nineteen, in college, and heading for trouble, as Annie's father always said.

Annie wanted to be a teacher.

"Are you excited?" Julia asked. "You think he's going to be there?"

"He," was Tim. He was the talk of the campus and the guy they all desired. He was tall, blond, and a quarterback. He was perfect. And he had his eye on Annie.

"I hope so," Annie said, and put on her jacket with the shoulder pads. "He asked me to come; he'd better be."

She looked at her friend, wondering why Tim hadn't chosen Julia instead. She was much prettier.

"Shall we?" Julia asked and opened the door. They were both wearing heavy make-up and acid-washed jeans.

Annie was nervous as they walked to the party. She had never been to a party in a fraternity house before. She had been thrilled when Tim came up to her in the library where she hung out most of the time and told her there was a party at the house and asked if she was going to come.

"Sure," she had replied, while blushing.

"This is it," Julia said, as they approached the house. Kids a few years older than them were hanging out on the porch, while loud music spilled out through the open windows. Annie had butterflies in her stomach as they went up the steps to the front of the house and entered, elbowing themselves through the crowd.

The noise was intense. People were drinking and smoking everywhere. Some were already making out on a couch. And it wasn't even nine o'clock yet.

"Let's get something to drink," Julia yelled through the thick clamor. "Have you loosen up a little."

Julia came back with two cups, and...Tim. "Look who I found," she said. "He was asking for you."

Annie grabbed the plastic cup and didn't care what it contained; she gulped it down in such a hurry she forgot to breathe. Tim was staring at her with that handsome smile of his. Then, he leaned over, put his hand on her shoulder, and whispered. "Glad you came."

Annie blushed and felt warmth spread through her entire body from the palm of Tim's hand on her shoulder. She really liked him. She really, really liked him.

"It's very loud in here. Do you want to go somewhere?" he asked.

Annie knew she wasn't the smartest among girls. Her mother had always told her so. She knew Tim, who was pre-med, would never be impressed with her conversational skills or her wits. If she was to dazzle him, it had to be in another way.

"Sure," she said.

"Let me get us some drinks first," Tim said and disappeared.

Julia smiled and grabbed Annie's shoulders. "You got him, girl." Then she corrected Annie's hair and wiped a smear of mascara from under her eyes.

"There. Now you're perfect. Remember. Don't think. You always overthink everything. Just be you. Just go with the flow, all right? Laugh at his jokes, but not too hard. Don't tell him too much about yourself; stay mysterious. And, whatever you do…don't sleep with him. You hear me? He won't respect you if you jump into bed with him right away. You have to play hard to get."

Annie stared at Julia. She had never had sex with anyone before, and she certainly wasn't going to now. Not yet. She had been saving herself for the right guy, and maybe Tim was it, but she wasn't going to decide that tonight. She didn't even want to.

"I'd never do that," she said with a scoff. "I'm not THAT stupid."

6

January 2015

W easel was standing outside the house as I drove up and parked the school bus on the street. The house on West Bay Drive was blocked by four police cars and lots of police tape. I saw several of my colleagues walking around in the yard. Weasel spotted me and approached. She was wearing tight black jeans, a belt with a big buckle, a white shirt, and black blazer. She looked to be in her thirties, but I knew she had recently turned forty.

"What the...?" she said with a grin, looking at the bus. She had that raspy rawness to her voice, and I always wondered if she could sing. I pictured her as a country singer. She gave out that tough vibe.

"Don't ask," I said. "What have we got?"

"Homicide," Weasel answered. "Victim is female. Laura Bennett, thirty-two, Mom of Ben, five years old. The husband's name is Brandon Bennett."

My heart dropped. I knew the boy. He was in the twins' class. I couldn't believe it. I had moved to Cocoa Beach from Miami in 2008 and never been called out to a homicide in my own town. Our biggest problems around here were usually tourists on spring break jumping in people's pools and Jacuzzis and leaving beer cans, or the youngsters having bonfires on the beach and burning people's chairs and leaving trash.

But, murder? That was a first for me in Cocoa Beach. I had been called out to drug related homicides in the beachside area before, but that was mostly further down south in Satellite Beach and Indialantic, but never this far up north.

"It's bad," Weasel said. "I have close to no experience with this type of thing, but you do. We need all your Miami-experience now. Show me what you've got."

I nodded and followed her into the house. It was located on a canal leading to the Banana River, like most of the houses on the back side of the island. The house had a big pebble-coated pool area with two waterfalls, a slide, and a spa overlooking the river. The perfect setting for Florida living, the real estate ad would say. With the huge palm trees, it looked like true paradise. Until you stepped inside.

The inside was pure hell.

It was a long time since I had been on a murder scene, but the Weasel was right. I was the only one with lots of experience in this field. I spent eight years in downtown Miami, covering Overtown, the worst neighborhood in the town, as part of the homicide unit. My specialty was the killer's psychology. I was a big deal back then. But when I met Arianna and she became pregnant with the twins, I was done. It was suddenly too dangerous. We left Miami to get away from it. We moved to Cocoa Beach, where my parents lived, to be closer to my family and to get away from murder.

Now, it had followed me here. It made me feel awful. I hated to see the town's innocence go like this.

My colleagues from the Cocoa Beach Police Department greeted me with nods as we walked through the living room, overlooking the yard with the pool. I knew all of them. They seemed a little confused. For most of them, it was a first. Officer Joel Hall looked pale.

"Joel was first man here," Weasel said.

"How are you doing, Joel?" I asked.

"Been better."

"So, tell me what happened."

Joel sniffled and wiped his nose on his sleeve.

"We got a call from the boy. He told us his mother had been killed. He found her finger…well, the dog had it in his mouth. He didn't dare to go upstairs. He called 911 immediately. I was on patrol close by, so I drove down here."

"So, what did you find?"

"The boy and the dog were waiting outside the house. He was hysterical, kept telling me his parents were dead. Then, he showed me the finger. I tried to calm him down and tell him I would go look and to stay outside. I walked up and found the mother…" Joel sniffled again. He took in a deep breath.

"Take your time, Joel," I said, and put my hand on his shoulder. Joel finally caved in and broke down.

"You better see it with your own eyes," Weasel said. "But brace yourself."

I followed her up the stairs of the house, where the medical examiners were already taking samples.

"The kid said his parents were dead. What about the dad?" I asked. "You only said one homicide."

"The dad's fine. But, hear this," Weasel said. "He claims he was asleep the entire time. He's been taken to the hospital to see a doctor. He kept claiming he felt dizzy and had blurred vision. I had to have a doctor look at him before we talk to him. The boy is with him. Didn't want to leave his side. The dog is there too. Jim and Marty took them there. I don't want him to run. He's our main suspect so far."

We walked down the hallway till we reached the bedroom. "Brace yourself," Weasel repeated, right before we walked inside.

I sucked in my breath. Then I froze.

"It looks like he was dismembering her," Weasel said. "He cut off all the fingers on her right hand, one by one, then continued on to the toes on her foot."

I felt disgusted by the sight. I held a hand to cover my mouth, not because it smelled, but because I always became sick to my stomach when facing a dead body. Especially one that was mutilated. I never got used to it. I kneeled next to the woman lying on the floor. I examined her face and eyes, lifted her eyelids, then looked closely at her body.

"There's hardly any blood. No bruises either," I said. "I say she was strangled first, then he did the dismembering. My guess is he was disturbed. He was about to cut her into bits and pieces, but he stopped."

I sniffed the body and looked at the Weasel, who seemed disgusted by my motion. "The kill might have happened in the shower. She has been washed recently. Maybe he drowned her."

I walked into the bathroom and approached the tub. I ran a finger along the sides. "Look." I showed her my finger. "There's still water on the sides. It's been used recently."

"So, you think she was killed in the bathtub? Strangulation, you say? But there are no marks on her neck or throat?"

"Look at her eyes. Petechiae. Tiny red spots due to ruptured capillaries. They are a signature injury of strangulation. She has them under the eyelids. He didn't use his hands. He was being gentle."

Weasel looked appalled. "Gentle? How can you say he was gentle? He cut off her fingers?"

"Yes, but look how methodical he was. All the parts are intact. Not a bruise on any of them. Not a drop of blood. They are all placed neatly next to one another. It's a declaration of love."

Weasel looked confused. She grumbled. "I don't see much love in any of all this, that's for sure. All I see is a dead woman, who someone tried to chop up. And now I want you to find out who did it."

I chuckled. "So, the dad tells us he was sleeping?" I asked.

Weasel shrugged. "Apparently, he was drunk last night. They had friends over. It got a little heavy, according to the neighbors. Loud music and loud voices. But that isn't new with these people."

"On a Sunday night in a nice neighborhood like this?" I asked, surprised.

"Apparently."

"It's a big house. Right on the river. Snug Harbor is one of the most expensive neighborhoods around here. What do the parents do for a living?"

"Nothing, I've been told. They live off the family's money. The deceased's father was a very famous writer. He died ten years ago. The kids have been living off of the inheritance and the royalties for years since."

"Anyone I know, the writer?"

"Probably," she said. "A local hero around here. John Platt."

"John Platt?" I said. "I've certainly heard of him. I didn't know he used to live around here. Wasn't he the guy who wrote all those thriller-novels that were made into movies later on?"

"Yes, that was him. He has sold more than 100 million books worldwide. His books are still topping the bestseller lists."

"Didn't he recently publish a new book or something?"

Weasel nodded. "They found an old unpublished manuscript of his on his computer, which they published. I never understood how those things work, but I figure they think, if he wrote it, then it's worth a lot of money even if he trashed it."

I stared at the dead halfway-dismembered body on the floor, then back at the Weasel.

I sighed. "I guess we better talk to this heavily sleeping dad first."

7

January 2015

"Who was that guy you talked to last night?"

Joe walked into the kitchen. Shannon was cutting up oranges to make juice. She sensed he was right behind her, but she didn't turn to look at him. Last night was still in her head. The humming noise of the voices, the music, the laughter. Her head was hurting from a little too much alcohol. His question made everything inside of her freeze.

"Who do you mean?" she asked. "I talked to a lot of people. That was kind of the idea with the party after my concert. For me to meet with the press and important people in the business. That's the way it always is. You know how it goes. It's a big part of my job."

He put his hand on her shoulder. A shiver ran up her spine. She closed her eyes.

Not now. Please not now.

"Look at me when you're talking to me," he said.

She took in a deep breath, then put on a smile; the same smile she used when the press asked her to pose for pictures, the same smile she put on for her manager, her record label, and her friends when they asked her about the bruises on her back, followed by the sentence:

"Just me being clumsy again."

Shannon turned and looked at Joe. His eyes were black with fury. Her body shrunk and her smile froze.

"I saw the way you were looking at that guy. Don't you think I saw that?" Joe asked. "You know what I think? I think you like going to these parties they throw in your honor. I think you enjoy all the men staring at you, wishing you were theirs, wanting to fuck your brains out. I see it in their eyes and I see it in yours as well. You like it."

It was always the same. Joe couldn't stand the fact that Shannon was the famous one…that she was the one everyone wanted to talk to, and after a party like the one yesterday, he always lost his temper with her. Because he felt left out, because there was no one looking at him, talking to him, asking him questions with interest. He hated the fact that Shannon was the one with a career, when all he had ever dreamt of was to be singing in sold out stadiums like she did.

They had started out together. Each with just a guitar under their arm, working small clubs and bars in Texas, then later they moved on to Nashville, where country musicians were made. They played the streets together, and then got small gigs in bars, and later small concert venues around town. But when a record label contacted them one day after a concert, they were only interested in her. They only wanted Shannon King. Since then, Joe had been living in the shadow of his wife, and that didn't become him well. For years, she had made excuses for him, telling herself he was going through a rough time; he was just hurting because he wasn't going anywhere with his music. The only thing Joe had going for him right now was the fact that he was stronger than Shannon.

But as the years had passed, it was getting harder and harder for her to come up with new excuses, new explanations. Especially now that they had a child together. A little girl who was beginning to ask questions.

"Joe…I…I don't know what you're talking about. I talked to a lot of people last night. I'm tired and now I really want to get some breakfast."

"Did you just take a tone with me. Did ya'? Am I so insignificant in your life that you don't even talk to me with respect, huh? You don't even look at me when we're at your precious after party. Nobody cares about me. Everyone just wants to talk to the *biiig* star, Shannon King," he said, mocking her.

"You're being ridiculous."

"Am I? Did you even think about me once last night? Did you? I left at eleven-thirty. You never even noticed. You never even texted me and asked where I was."

Shannon blushed. He was right. She hadn't thought about him even once. She had been busy answering questions from the press and talking about her tour. Everyone had been pulling at her; there simply was no time to think about him. Why couldn't he understand that?

"I thought so," Joe said. Then, he slapped her.

Shannon went stumbling backward against the massive granite counter. She hurt her back in the fall. Shannon whimpered, then got up on her feet again with much effort. Her cheek burned like hell. A little blood ran from the corner of her mouth. She wiped it off.

Careful what you say, Shannon. Careful not to upset him further. Remember what happened last time. He's not well. He is hurting. Careful not to hurt him any more.

But she knew it was too late. She knew once he crossed that line into that area where all thinking ceased to exist, it was too late. She could appeal to his sensitivity as much as she wanted to. She could try and explain herself and tell him she was sorry, but it didn't help. If anything, it only made everything worse.

His eyes were bulging and his jaws clenched. His right eye had that tick in it that only showed when he was angry.

You got to get out of here.

"Joe, please, I…"

A fist throbbed through the air and smashed into her face.

Quick. Run for the phone.

She could see it. It was on the breakfast bar. She would

have to spring for it. Shannon jumped to the side and managed to avoid his next fist, then slipped on the small rug on the kitchen floor, got back up in a hurry, and rushed to reach out for the phone.

Call 911. Call the police.

Her legs were in the air and she wasn't running anymore. He had grabbed her by the hair, and now he was pulling her backwards. He yanked her towards him, and she screamed in pain, cursing her long blonde hair that she used to love so much…that the world loved and put on magazine covers.

"You cheating lying bitch!" he screamed, while pulling her across the floor.

He lifted her up, then threw her against the kitchen counter. It blew out the air from her lungs. She couldn't scream anymore. She was panting for air and wheezing for him to stop. She was bleeding from her nose. Joe came closer, then leaned over her and, with his hand, he corrected his hair. His precious hair that had always meant so much to him, that he was always fixing and touching to make sure it was perfect, which it ironically never was.

"No one disrespects me. Do you hear me? Especially not you. You're a nobody. Do you understand? You would be nothing if it wasn't for me," he yelled, then lifted his clenched fist one more time. When it smashed into Shannon's face again and again, she finally let herself drift into a darkness so deep she couldn't feel anything anymore.

8

January 2015

"Hi there. Ben, is it?" I asked.

The boy was sitting next to his dad in the hospital bed, the dog sleeping by his feet.

"He won't leave his dad's side," Marty said.

Ben looked up at me with fear in his eyes. "It's okay, Ben," I said, and kneeled in front of him. "We can talk here."

"I know you," Ben said. "You're Austin and Abigail's dad."

"That's right. And you're in their class. I remember you. Say, weren't you supposed to be at the zoo today?"

Ben nodded with a sad expression.

"Well, there'll be other times," I said. I paused while Ben looked at his father, who was sleeping.

"He's completely out cold," Marty said. "He was complaining that he couldn't control his arms and legs, had spots before his eyes, and he felt dizzy and nauseated. Guess it was really heavy last night."

I looked at the very pale dad. "Or maybe it was something else," I said.

"What do you mean?"

I looked closer at the dad.

"Did you talk to him?"

"Only a few words. When I asked about last night, he kept

saying he didn't remember what happened, that he didn't know where he was. He kept asking me what time it was. Even after I had just told him."

"Hm."

"What?" Marty asked.

"Did they run his blood work?" I asked.

"No. I told them it wasn't necessary. He was just hung over. The doctor looked at him quickly and agreed. We agreed to let him to sleep it off. He seemed like he was still drunk when he talked to us."

"Is my dad sick, Mr. Ryder?" Ben asked.

I looked at the boy and smiled. "No, son, but I am afraid your dad has been poisoned."

"Poisoned?" Marty asked. "What on earth do you mean?"

"Dizziness, confusion, blurry vision, difficulty talking, nausea, difficulty controlling your movements all are symptoms of Rohypnol poisoning. Must have been ingested to have this big of an effect. Especially with alcohol."

"Roofied?" Marty laughed. "Who on earth in their right mind would give a grown man a rape drug?"

"Someone who wanted to kill him and his wife," I said.

I walked into the hallway and found a nurse and asked her to make sure they tested Brandon Bennett for the drug in his blood. Then, I called the medical examiner and told them to check the wife's blood as well. Afterwards, I returned to talk to Ben.

"So, Ben, I know this is a difficult time for you, but I would be really happy if you could help me out by talking a little about last night. Can you help me out here?"

Ben wiped his eyes and looked at me. His face was swollen from crying. Then he nodded. I opened my arms. "Come here, buddy. You look like you could use a good bear hug."

Ben hesitated, then looked at his dad, who was still out cold, before he finally gave in and let me hug him. I held him in my arms, the way I held my own children when they were sad. The boy finally cried.

"It's okay," I whispered. "Your dad will be fine."

My words felt vague compared to what the little boy had seen this morning, how his world had been shaken up. His dad was probably going to be fine, but he would never see his mother again, and the real question was whether the boy would ever be fine again?

He wept in my arms for a few minutes, then pulled away and wiped his nose on his sleeve. "Do you promise to catch the guy that killed my mother?" he asked.

I sighed. "I can promise I'll do my best. How about that?"

Ben thought about it for a little while, then nodded with a sniffle.

"Okay. What do you want to know?" he asked.

"Who came to your house last night? I heard your parents had guests. Who were they?"

9

April 1984

Tim took Annie down to the lake behind campus, where they sat down. The grass was moist from the sprinklers. Annie felt self-conscious with the way Tim stared at her. It was a hot night out. The cicadas were singing; Annie was sweating in her small dress. Her skin felt clammy.

Tim finally broke the silence.

"Has anyone ever told you how incredibly beautiful you are?"

Annie's head was spinning from her drink. The night was intoxicating, the sounds, the smell, the moist air hugging her. She shook her head. Her eyes stared at the grass. She felt her cheeks blushing.

"No."

"Really?" Tim said. "I find that very hard to believe."

Annie giggled, then sipped her drink. She really liked Tim. She could hardly believe she was really here with him.

"Look at the moon," he said and pointed.

It was a full moon. It was shining almost as bright as daylight. Its light hit the lake. Annie took in a deep breath, taking in the moment.

"It's beautiful," she said with a small still voice. She was afraid of talking too much, since he would only realize she wasn't smart, and then he might regret being with her.

Just go with the flow.

"I loathe Florida," Tim said. "I hate these warm nights. I hate how sweaty I always am. I'm especially sick of Orlando. When I'm done here, I'm getting out of this state. I wanna go up north. Don't you?"

Annie shrugged. She had lived all her life in Florida. Thirty minutes north of Orlando, to be exact. Born and raised in Windermere. Her parents still lived there, and that was where she was planning on going back once she had her degree. Annie had never thought about going anywhere else.

"I guess it's nice up north as well," she said, just to please him.

Tim laughed, then looked at her with those intense eyes once again. It made her uncomfortable. But part of her liked it as well. A big part.

"Can I kiss you?" he asked.

Annie blushed. She really wanted him to. Then she nodded. Tim smiled, then leaned over and put his lips on top of hers. Annie felt the dizziness from the drink. It was buzzing in her head. The kiss made her head spin, and when Tim pressed her down on the moist grass, she let him. He crawled on top of her, and with deep moans kept kissing her lips, then her cheeks, her ears, and her neck. Annie felt like laughing because it tickled so much, but she held it back to not ruin anything. Tim liked her and it made her happy.

"Boy, you're hot," he said, groaning, as he kissed her throat and moved further down her body. He grinned and started to open her dress, taking one button at a time. Annie felt insecure. What was he going to do next?

Tim pulled the dress open and looked at her bra, then he ripped it off.

"Ouch," Annie said. She tried to cover her breasts with her arms, but Tim soon grabbed them and pulled them to her sides. He held her down while kissing her breasts. He groaned while sucking on her nipples. Annie wasn't sure if she liked it or not. He was being a little rough, and she was afraid of going too far with him.

Whatever you do, don't sleep with him. No matter what.

"Stop," she mumbled, when he pulled the dress off completely and grabbed her panties. Tim stopped. He stared at Annie. She felt bad. Had she scared him away? Was he ever going to see her again if she didn't let him?

No matter what.

No. She wasn't ready for this. She had saved herself. This wasn't how it was supposed to happen. Not like this. Not here.

"I want to go home," Annie said.

Tim smiled and tilted his head, then leaned over and whispered in her ear. "Not yet, sweetheart, not yet."

He stroked her face gently and kissed her cheeks, while she fought and tried to get him off her body. In the distance, she heard voices, and soon she felt hands on her body, hands touching her, hands slapping her face. She felt so dizzy and everything became a blur of faces, laughing voices, cheering voices, hands everywhere, groping her, touching her, hurting her. And then the pain followed.

The excruciating pain.

10

January 2015

B randon Bennett was still out cold when I had to leave the hospital. I decided to wait to interrogate him till later. Ben had told me that he had been asleep, so he hadn't seen who was at the house, but there were two of his parents' neighbors who usually came over to drink with his mom and dad. I got the names and called for both of them to come into the station in the afternoon. Meanwhile, I had to drive back to the zoo to pick up the kids and get them back to their school.

"Daddy!" my kids yelled when I opened the doors to the school bus and they stormed in, screaming with joy. Both of them clung to my neck.

"How was the zoo?" I asked.

"So much fun!" Abigail exclaimed. She was the most outgoing of the two, and often the one who spoke for them. I had a feeling Austin was the thinker, the one who would turn out to be a genius some day. Well, maybe not exactly a genius, but there was something about him. Abigail was the one who came up with all their naughty plans, and she always got Austin in on them.

"Good. I'm glad," I said and smooched their cheeks loudly.

"You would have loved it, Dad," Abigail continued. "You should have come. What was so important anyway?"

I exhaled and kissed her again, then let go of her. "Just some work thing. Nothing to worry about."

The twins looked at each other. Abigail placed her hands on her hips and looked at me with her head tilted.

"What?" I asked.

"You only say for us to not worry if there is actually something to worry about," Abigail said. "Am I right?" She looked at Austin, who nodded.

"She's right, Dad."

I smiled. "Well, it is nothing smart little noses like yours should get into, so get in the back of the bus with your friends and sit down. We're leaving now."

Abigail grumbled something, then grabbed her brother's shirt and they walked to the back. The bus gave a deep sigh when I closed the doors and we took off.

The atmosphere on the bus driving back was loud and very cheerful. Loudest of all were my twins, but this time I didn't mind too much. After the morning I had spent with a dead body and a poor kid who had lost his mother, I was just so pleased that my kids were still happy and innocent. They didn't look at me with that empty stare in their eyes, the one where you know they'll never trust the world again. That broken look that made them appear so much older than they were.

"Grandma and Grandpa will pick you up," I said, as I dropped them off at Roosevelt Elementary School.

"Yay!" they both exclaimed.

I told their teacher as well, then parked the bus and gave the keys back to the front office.

"Thank you so much for helping out today," Elaine at the desk said. "It's always wonderful when the parents get involved."

"Anytime," I said.

I walked to my car, a red Jeep Convertible. I got in and drove to the station with the top down. I bought my favorite sandwich at Juice 'N Java Café, called Cienna. It had a Porto-bello mushroom, yellow tomato, goat cheese arugula, and pesto on Pugliese bread. I figured I had earned it after the morning I had.

The police station was located inside of City Hall, right in the heart of Cocoa Beach. I knew the place well, even though I was usually located at the sheriff's offices in Rockledge. Cocoa Beach was my town, and every time they needed a detective, I was the one they called for. Even if they were cases that didn't involve homicide. As I entered through the glass doors, Weasel came towards me. Two officers flanked her.

"Going out for lunch?" I asked.

"Yes. I see you've already gotten yours," she said, nodding at my bag with my sandwich from the café.

"I'm expecting two of the neighbors in for questioning in a short while. Any news I should know about?" I asked.

Weasel sighed. "The ME has taken the body in for examination. They expect to have the cause of death within a few hours, they say. They're still working on the house."

"Any fingerprints so far?"

"Lots. We asked around a little and heard the same story from most of the neighbors. The Bennetts were a noisy bunch. Nothing that has ever been reported, but the wife and husband fought a lot, one neighbor told us. He said they yelled and screamed at each other when they got drunk. He figured the husband finally had enough. I guess it sounds plausible. He killed her, then panicked and tried to dismember her body to get rid of it. But the dog interrupted him. He decided to pretend he had been asleep through the whole thing. When we arrived, the dad was asleep when Joel went up, but he might have pretended to be. Joel said he seemed out of it, though. Might just be a good actor."

"It's all a lot of theories so far," I said with a deep exhale. It was going to be a long day for me. I was so grateful I had my parents nearby.

I grew up in Ft. Lauderdale, further down south, but

when I left for college, my parents wanted to try something new. They bought a motel by the beach in Cocoa Beach a few years after I left the house. The place was a haven for the kids. They never missed me while they were there. That made it easier for me to work late.

"I've cleared an office for you," Weasel said. "We're glad to have you here to help us."

I put a hand on her broad shoulder. "Likewise. I'll hold down the fort. Enjoy your lunch."

11

January 2015

"It all started when they lost their daughter."

It was late in the afternoon at the station. I had interviewed two of the neighbors who usually came to the Bennetts' house to drink with them, but hadn't gotten anything out of them. They didn't even know the Bennetts very well, they told me. They just knew that there was free booze. The Bennetts were loaded, and every drunk in the neighborhood knew that they could always find a party there. Only one of the two, Travis Connor, had been at the Bennett's house the night before. He told us he was the only guest at the time, but he hadn't stayed long. He had left the house at ten o'clock and gone to the Beach Shack to hang out with some buddies. I called, and they confirmed his alibi. The next-door neighbor, Mrs. Jeffries had told my colleagues that she had seen Laura Bennett walk onto the back porch at eleven to smoke a cigarette. So, I let the guy go. His hands were shaking heavily, and I guessed he was in a hurry to find a drink somewhere.

Around three o'clock, a woman had come to the station and asked to talk to someone about the killing of Laura Bennett. Her name was Gabrielle Phillips.

The front desk sent her to me. Now, I was sitting across from her as she explained why she had come.

"They lost their child last year, and that's when it all went wrong," she continued. "I've known Laura since high school," she said. "She never used to drink. But when their daughter died in her bed at night, everything changed."

"Sudden Infant Death Syndrome?" I asked, and wrote it on a notepad.

"Yes. After that, they started drinking. Well, to be honest, Brandon has always drunk a lot, but she never did. Never touched a drop. It wasn't her thing. She didn't like to lose control."

"So, they drank and partied because they lost their child?" I asked.

"Well, Brandon always liked to party. Especially after Laura inherited all that money. He didn't have to work anymore. He had always liked to drink, but it got really bad. She was actually considering leaving him and taking the kids, but then the daughter died in her sleep, and she couldn't take it. She had a drink and then never stopped again. I tried to talk to her, but she shut me out and told me it was none of my business."

Gabrielle looked upset. I could tell she had loved her friend and cared for her. She was choking up, but held back the tears.

"I tried…" she continued. "I really did. But she wouldn't listen to me. I told her that guy was all wrong for her. He was trouble from the beginning."

I reached behind me and grabbed a box of tissues that I handed to her. She grabbed it and wiped her eyes, careful not to smear her make-up. I wrote on my notepad and tried to get all the details down.

"So, you say she inherited a lot of money? From her dad, right?" I asked.

"She inherited ten million dollars from him, and she never even knew him."

I looked up. "Excuse me?"

"She was born outside of marriage. Her mother was an affair that John Platt had once when he was on a book tour.

They met in Tampa, where she lived at the time. Nine months later, Laura was born. John Platt refused to have anything to do with the child. He paid a good amount of money to the mother to keep her mouth shut and never tell the child who her real father was. Laura's mother later remarried when Laura was still a baby, and they decided to have the new husband be the father as well. To prevent any awkward questions. And to have Laura grow up with a real family. Her new father loved her, and she still looks at him like her real father. Both of her parents died two years ago in a car accident outside of Orlando."

"Sounds like Laura has suffered a lot of loss the last couple of years," I said.

Gabrielle sniffled and wiped her nose in a ladylike manner.

"So, her husband Brandon, tell me more about him?"

"He is the scum of the earth," Gabrielle hissed. "But, somehow, she loved him."

"How did they meet?"

"At a sports game. Can you believe it? A baseball game. UCF Knights were playing South Florida. Laura went to UCF; Brandon had just come to watch the game with some friends. He was an auto mechanic and smelled like oil and trouble, if you ask me. Smoked and drank too much. Liked to party. I was with her on the night they met outside the stadium. He just walked right up to her and told her she was gorgeous and that he would like to invite her out sometime. I was surprised to hear her accept. I couldn't believe her. But I guess she somehow wanted to rebel against her parents or something. They never liked him either, but she married him anyway. After four months of them dating, he proposed. Four months! I knew she was going to get herself in trouble with this guy. I just knew it."

"So, tell me some more about the inheritance. When did she realize she was going to get all this money?"

"It was right before the pig proposed. Go figure, right? He heard about the money, then wanted to marry her. I couldn't believe she didn't see it, but she told me she loved him, and I really think she did. I think all he loved was her money. Anyway, that's just my opinion."

"How did she learn about the money? From a lawyer?" I asked, thinking it must have been quite a shock…suddenly being a millionaire and suddenly realizing your entire childhood was based on a lie.

Gabrielle shook her head and wiped her nose again. She drank from the glass of water I had placed in front of her. It was hot outside. In the low eighties. She was wearing shorts and flip-flops. The state costume of Florida. Even in January.

"No, it was the strangest thing. He called her."

"Who?"

"John Platt. He called her right before he died. How he got her number, I don't know, but I guess when you're that big you have people working for you. He was sick, he said. Cancer was eating him and he wanted her to come. He didn't tell her why, only that he had something for her. At first, Laura thought it was a joke, but he gave her an address and she looked it up and it turned out to be right. She called me afterwards and told me everything. She was freaking out. Said she had decided she didn't want to go, because it was too weird. But I convinced her to do it. I went with her, so she wouldn't be alone. Together, we were invited into his huge mansion on the beach in Cocoa Beach. He told her he was happy to see her. There were others there. I later learned they were her siblings. Two sisters and a brother. They had all grown up in the house, but were now living on their own, except for the youngest, who hadn't left the house yet, even though he was in his mid-twenties. They weren't very happy to see her, I can tell you that much. They weren't prepared to share their inheritance with some stranger, but they soon learned they had to."

"So, what happened?" I asked "What did John Platt tell her?"

"It was such an awkward scene. He was lying in bed, surrounded by nurses and family. He teared up when he saw

43

Laura. It made her really uncomfortable. He wanted to hold her hand and started to cry. Then, he handed her a piece of paper. *Take this,* he said. *You deserve this more than any of the others."*

"So, what was written on the paper?"

"It was a will. He had changed his will a few hours before we arrived. His lawyer had signed it and everything. It stated that she was going to inherit everything. All he had. The house, his money, everything."

I leaned back in my chair while the story came together for me. "So, the siblings didn't get anything?"

She shook her head. "Nope. Not a dime. They had grown up in luxury, so their father figured it was time for them to learn how to earn a decent living on their own. That's what he wrote in the letter. Laura had never known who her father was, never had any of his money, now he was giving her everything. I guess he tried to make amends for not letting her know he was her dad all those years. Laura was baffled, to put it mildly. She read the letter, but didn't understand. How could he be her father? She already had a father. She ran out of the house crying, and I ran after her. John Platt died shortly after, we later learned. Good thing for him, I think. Otherwise, the siblings would probably have started a riot. They tried to fight Laura with all their big lawyers afterwards, trying to declare that their dad was dying, and therefore not in his right mind when he made the will. After several months of going back and forth, the judge decided they didn't have a case and closed it. Laura was rich and, in time, came to accept the fact that she had been the result of an affair. Her mother confirmed it was true, and they didn't speak for a long time, but she forgave her eventually. Laura and Brandon bought the house in Snug Harbor and moved here shortly after they were married. She sold John Platt's old house, but wanted to stay in the town. She liked it here, she told me. I didn't see her much after she moved, since I live north of Orlando now, and I work full time, but every now and then, we would meet and catch up. But she was never really happy. She had Ben, and he was the joy of her life, but she kept talking about how Brandon was drinking and gambling her money away on the casino boats, acting like this big shot with her money. She wanted to leave him, but then she was pregnant again and decided to stay for the children. I met with her the week before the baby died. She said she was going to leave him, this time for real. That she was going back to the Tampa area and start over with the kids. Brandon's drinking had gotten worse, and he was still gambling a lot. In a few years, he had spent more than a third of her money. She was still certain he loved her, and maybe he does. I don't know him well enough to say he doesn't. But he also loved the money, and that's what went so wrong. After the baby died, I went to the funeral and Laura had a black eye. She told me in confidence that Brandon had slapped her, that he blamed her for the child's death. They fought about that a lot, she told me. He couldn't believe she hadn't checked on the baby during the night. It was her fault, he told her. And she believed him. She felt so guilty, she told me. So much it hurt. I said she should leave him, that now was the time to go, and she agreed, but she never did. Instead, she lowered herself to his level and took up drinking. The last time I spoke to her was three months ago, and she was so drunk on the phone I could hardly understand what she was saying. Now…I can't believe she's gone. What's to become of Ben?"

I shook my head with a deep exhale. I was starting to wonder that myself.

12

January 2015

S hannon heard her daughter's voice calling in the distance. Then the door slammed and the voice came closer, even though it was all still drowned in a heavy daze.

"Moom? Moom?" the voice became shrill and clearer.

Shannon tried to blink her eyes to be able to see, but it hurt too much.

She felt a hand in hers, then someone pulling her arm.

"Mom? Please, wake up, Mom, please?"

Shannon growled something, trying to speak, but her lip hurt. She blinked again, and soon an image emerged of her daughter looking at her with terrified eyes.

"Mom, are you all right? Speak to me, Mommy!"

You gotta say something. The girl is scared. Seeing you like this. Say something to calm her down.

Shannon opened her eyes wide and looked at her daughter. Her beautiful Angela. The love of her life. The only beautiful thing in her life. The one thing she had done right.

"Hi, sweetie."

"Mommy. What happened? Are you hurt?"

With much effort, Shannon sat up on the kitchen floor. She leaned her head on the cupboards behind her. So much pain.

"Mommy must have fallen," she said, and felt blood on her fingers when she touched her face.

"Again?" Angela said.

"Yeah. Again."

"You're so clumsy, Mommy," Angela said. She grabbed a towel and wet it. Then she put ice cubes inside of it and handed it to Shannon. She did it with such expertise and experience that it terrified Shannon.

"Thanks, sweetie," she said.

"Where is Daddy?" Angela asked. "Do you want me to call him?"

"No. No. Don't disturb him. I'm fine. Really. I just need to…to rest my head a little bit."

Angela sat down next to her. "I've been thinking," she said with that grown-up voice of hers.

Too grown-up for a six-year-old.

"Maybe you shouldn't be left at home alone anymore. You get hurt all the time. I think it would be best if there was someone with you. Last week it was the stairs, remember?"

Shannon drew in a deep breath. She remembered too well. And so did Angela, apparently. She was getting too old. It wouldn't be long before she figured out what was really going on.

Did you really think you could hide it from her forever?

She didn't. But she had hoped it would get better with time. She had hoped Joe would get better, that it would all blow over and he would stop being so angry with her. For a long time, she had tried to change it by changing herself, by being nicer and staying away from things that made him angry, but now she knew it didn't matter how she behaved. It wasn't going to change.

"You know what? Maybe you're right," she said. "Maybe you and I should take a trip somewhere soon. What do you say?"

Angela's face lit up. "That sounds awesome, Mom."

Shannon sighed and grabbed the edge of the kitchen counter. She pulled herself up, while her daughter tried to help her. She had been thinking about doing this for many months. Now was the time.

"I better go do my homework," Angela said, and jumped for the stairs.

Shannon stopped her halfway up. "Hey, sweetie."

"Yes, Mom?"

"Not a word to Dad, all right? Not a word about the trip, okay?"

She nodded while biting her lip.

She knows. Oh, God, she knows, doesn't she?

"All right, Mom."

13

January 2015

I t was dark before I made it back to the motel to pick up the kids. I had missed dinnertime, but my mom had made a plate for me that she heated in the microwave of the small restaurant that was attached to the motel.

The place was called Motel Albert. They had named it after my dad, Albert Ryder, since it was his big dream that had come true. It was located right between A1A and the beach. The rooms were small, but not too shabby. The restaurant at the end of the building had a deck on the beach side where people could sit, have a hotdog or a fish burger, and watch the waves and the dolphins if they were lucky. I loved the place and so did my kids. They could play on the beach for hours and hours nonstop. They were like fish in the water, and I had slowly started to teach them how to surf as well. Abigail was by far the better of them, since she was the daredevil and never afraid of anything, whereas Austin was a lot more careful type. Emily refused to even try, but I kept asking her anyway. At sixteen years of age, everything is lame, apparently. I wasn't giving up on her, though. I had surfed all of my life, and I wanted all of them to have the gift of surfing in their lives as well. I never missed a good swell. The waves in Ft. Lauderdale, where I grew up, weren't as good as they were here in Cocoa Beach. This was heaven for me, and I hoped it would be for my kids as well.

"Tough day, huh?" my mom, Sherri Ryder, asked when I reached for a second portion of fish tacos. She had made them herself, and there was no better on the beach. She knew I couldn't stop eating when I had a lot on my mind. I used to be a lot bigger when I worked back in Miami. Since I moved to Cocoa Beach I had lost around twenty pounds, just because I surfed more and ate healthier. Plus, I rarely stressed, so I didn't overeat. I wasn't in the best shape of my life, but it was getting a lot better. I looked good, I believed. Still had all of my hair, even though my mom thought it was too long and curly for a man in the force.

"Yes," I said. "I mean, I know this stuff happens everywhere; it's just so shocking to see it here in Cocoa Beach."

I sipped my beer, made by the local brewery that my mother had a deal with. I enjoyed the local beers. I had one more. The twins came rushing towards me, closely followed by their granddad, who was skipping to keep up with them. He became such a child around them. It amused me. At the age of seventy-five, he was still very agile. He had always taken very good care of his body. He'd been running for most of his life. I hadn't been good to myself over the years. I hoped to have half of his health in ten years.

"Daaad!" they yelled.

I looked at my dad, who was smiling from ear to ear. There was nothing in this world he enjoyed more than spending time with the twins. "They're too fast," he said panting. "We were playing tag in the back, and I can't catch them."

I laughed and made room for him to sit next to me on the wooden bench. We were sitting outside on the porch, overlooking the dark ocean. The sun had set an hour ago, but I could hear the waves. They were picking up. We were supposed to get a really big swell later in the week. I, for one, hoped I could get time to catch some.

"Where's Emily?" I asked.

"She's in the TV room watching some show I don't under-stand half of," my mom said. "Why are vampires such a big deal now?"

I chuckled and shook my head. "I don't know, Mom."

"Anyway, she says you let her watch it, but I really don't think young girls should watch things like that."

"It's her thing, Mom. Let her," I said.

My mother didn't look like she wanted to. "I'm just saying it," she said shaking her head. "She needs to know how to be careful what she fills herself with."

"So, you had a tough day, I hear?" My dad interrupted. "We saw it on the news."

I nodded while removing some lettuce from between my teeth. "Yeah, I noticed the choppers earlier. I bet they're all over it."

"What about that poor kid?" my mom asked. "How is he ever going to get through life?"

It was typical of my mother to think about the kid. Kids had been her whole life. She was a kindergarten teacher for twenty-something years and adored all children. A lot more than she adored adults.

I wondered how much they had said about the case on the news. Had they told people that the body was partly dismem-bered? Weasel had been in charge of making the statements and had called for a press conference the next day. At City Hall, they were terrified that this was going to affect tourism. I couldn't blame them. The tourists meant everything around here. Especially at this time of year. The snowbird season. It meant jobs. It meant security for people. Ever since they stopped the Space Shuttle program, thousands of people had lost their jobs and the real estate market had plummeted. People lost a lot of money on their houses. They recently started a new project out at the Space Center, and they were still launching rockets every now and then, but the area had been bleeding for years. It wasn't only people who worked on the shuttle that were hurt. Everyone else was too. Hundreds thousands of tourists would usually come to watch a launch, and that meant a lot of money for the hotels, the restaurants, and shops. It helped a little that the cruise ships were booming, but the prices on houses were low, and lots of people were still out of work. My parents had felt it too. They used to have the motel packed several times a year when a shuttle was launched, and now they barely made ends meet.

"I don't know, Mom," I said and finished my beer. "We can only hope for the best."

"You'll catch him," my mom said. "You'll get the guy, and then everything will go back to normal again."

I chuckled. My mother had such great confidence in me; it was sweet. She never did like the fact that I was a detective or on the police force. Especially not when I worked in Miami. She feared for my life every day. I couldn't blame her. I didn't want any of my kids in the force either. But I happened to like my job. Not today, but most days.

14

January 2015

"I think we'll head home now," I said, and kissed my mom on the cheek. "Thanks for dinner; it was great, as always."

"We need to change a light bulb in room one-eleven. Could you do that before you leave? You know how your dad is with ladders. I don't like him climbing on them."

"I got it," I said.

I found a new bulb in the cupboard behind the bar, then grabbed the ladder and went into room one-eleven and changed it. I did all I could to help out around the motel. My parents were getting older, and it was harder and harder for them to keep up with the maintenance. It was the least I could do, with all the help they gave me. As my way of saying thanks, I devoted my weekends to helping them out. That way, the kids got to play with their grandparents too, so it was a win-win.

I looked at the twins, who were drawing on one of the tables in the restaurant. They were sitting underneath it and drawing on the bottom. Luckily, my parents hadn't noticed. I cleared my throat.

"Abigail, Austin. We need to go home. Emily?" I called through the window.

"What?" she answered.

"We're going home."

"Finally," she said.

I heard the TV shut off, then the sound of her dragging feet across the ground. She came out. She looked odd with her big army-boots and black outfit in this heat.

I smiled. "How was your day?"

She shrugged indifferently. "Fine, I guess." She grabbed her backpack and put it on. I wanted to give her a hug, but was afraid it would come off as awkward. Instead, I turned to face the twins. "I said we were leaving."

"Aw, we were having so much fun," Abigail said.

Austin crawled out from under the table and walked to me. "It wasn't my idea," he said, and handed me the crayon. "I know," I said. "Abigail. Get out from under there, now, young lady."

"Wait a second. I just need to finish this."

Was she kidding me?

"Abigail. Now."

She sighed and rolled her eyes. Six years of age and already a teenager. "All right, all right. I'm coming."

We walked to the car and greeted one of the guests of the motel. Harry was his name. He had been a guest for a month or so now. A snowbird. We had a lot of those. They came down from the north and stayed all winter.

"Nice evening?" I said, as we passed him.

He nodded and smiled at the children. "Yes, indeed. Gonna be a beautiful day tomorrow, don't you think?"

"Definitely."

No one discussed the weather as much as snowbirds. They came to keep warm in the winter, while the snow and cold roamed up north and made it miserable for people. Harry petted the children on their heads, then went on towards the beach. An older couple, Mr. and Mrs. Miller, who were also regulars and came every winter, got out of their car and walked towards the rooms. I nodded in greeting as I passed them, and we talked about the weather as well before they disappeared into their room. I was so happy for people like Harry and the Millers. They were the ones who let my parents earn enough money to be able to keep the motel.

I put the kids in the car and drove next door to the place where I had rented a condo. It was also right on the beach, and in walking distance of my parents' place. It was in South Cocoa Beach, in the more secluded part of town. I, for one, loved it here. Arianna hadn't liked it much. She thought it was too small…nothing really happened here, she always said.

That was what I liked about it.

"Can we watch TV before we go to bed, Dad, please?" Abigail asked with big pleading eyes.

"Okay," I said, as we walked towards the complex. I opened the front door and let the munchkins storm in and fight over who should hit the button for the elevator. "But only for half an hour," I said on the way up, when they had finally quieted down. Abigail had naturally won the fight. She always did. She was the big sister and had beat her brother into this world by fifty-eight seconds. She had been beating him ever since.

"Aw," Abigail pleaded. "Can't we say one hour instead?"

I sighed and opened the door to the condo. I looked at my watch. It was going to be late. "Okay." I said. "If you brush your teeth and put on your PJs first."

The kids didn't hear that last part before they stormed inside and threw themselves on the couch and turned the TV on. Emily went to her room and shut the door without a word, while the theme song to SpongeBob filled the living room. Each of the twins grabbed an iPad and started playing while watching TV.

The new generation of multitaskers.

I shook my head and sat next to them, and soon after, the iPads were put away and I had both kids on my lap.

15

September 1984

S he never told anyone what had happened to her. She was too ashamed, too scared of what would happen if she did. So, Annie kept it to herself. She didn't remember much. She couldn't recall the details, but she believed she had been raped. She just wasn't sure if it had all been a dream. She had woken up in the grass by the lake the next morning, but hadn't been able to remember what had happened. But, as the days passed, little by little, she remembered bits and pieces. She knew she had been with Tim. And she knew she was badly bruised when she woke up. She covered the marks with make-up and stayed away from her friends for weeks afterwards. She even avoided Julia and told her she wasn't feeling well. She didn't want to have to answer her questions. She didn't want anyone to know how stupid she had been.

She was determined to forget everything.

And she had succeeded. After the bruises were gone, no one ever asked questions or wondered what had happened. Except Julia…and Annie simply kept avoiding her. She missed her friendship like crazy, but she had to cut her off. That was the only way she could forget, the only way she could avoid having to talk about that night, that dreadful night when Tim had taken her to the lake.

But, as the fall came, something started to happen to Annie's body. It was like it had gotten a life of its own, like she had no control over it anymore.

She could wake up at night and suddenly be so hungry it felt like she was about to die if she didn't eat. She would keep crackers and candy under her pillow, so her roommate wouldn't wake up when she ate at night. She had a jar of pickles that she ate greedily. And then there was the extra weight. The nightly eating made her gain a lot of weight. And some nights her stomach would hurt. She even started throwing up in the mornings, and wondered if that was due to her strange hours of eating.

Finally, she went to the doctor and was examined. Her mother took her. She had come for a visit, and when Annie had thrown up for the third time while she was there, she suspected something was wrong.

"She's gaining weight rapidly," her mother told the doctor.

"Well, that's not too odd, given her circumstances," he said with a smile. "Congratulations."

Annie's mother shrieked. She went completely pale, then hid her face between her hands. "I feared it might be something like this," she said with a trembling voice.

On the way back to the campus, her mother didn't speak while driving. Not until she parked in front of the dorm. Annie felt sick to her stomach and a thousand thoughts went through her mind.

Was it Tim's? There were others that night. Could it be from one of them?

Her mother turned her head and looked at her. "Listen to me. I don't know who got you into this trouble," she said hissing. "But either you get married, or you have an abortion. You hear me? Or you'll never be able to set foot in our house again. You won't be our daughter anymore."

"But...but..."

Her mother turned her head away. "Fix this," she said. "Or don't come back home."

And just like that, Annie's life was changed forever. Standing in the parking lot, looking after her mother driving away, she knew nothing would ever be the same again. Her plan of becoming a teacher and going back to Windermere to teach at her old school, then marrying a nice guy and having a family was completely broken. Destroyed in a matter of seconds. She had no idea what to do, but she did know one thing. There was no way she was getting rid of the baby. She had heard stories of women not being able to conceive again. She was no killer. She could never kill a child. Born or unborn.

No way.

16

January 2015

The next morning, I watched the sun rise while sitting on my board. Emily had her own car that I had bought for her, and she took care of herself in the morning, so I took just the twins with me to my parents' place to eat breakfast. Meanwhile, I decided to start the day my favorite way, in the ocean. My mother had told me she would take the kids to the school bus, which stopped right outside the motel.

It was one of those unbelievably gorgeous mornings, where the sun was allowed to rise on a cloud free sky. The water was cold at this time of year, the coldest it got in Florida. I know people in other parts of the country would laugh at me thinking sixty-nine degree water was chilly, but to me it was. You get used to it being in the eighties for most parts of the year. So, I had put on my wetsuit and was waiting for the next wave, while wondering about Laura Bennett. I couldn't stop thinking about her and hadn't slept much all night. I kept going back to the way the killer had arranged the fingers after he had separated them from her body. They had all been in a neat row and so carefully cut off, like he didn't want to ruin them any more than necessary.

The waves rolled in in nice straight lines. They weren't big today, but the wind was off-shore, and they were glassy and smooth as I rode them on my longboard. The wind blew the top of the waves off as they broke, and created rainbows in the rays from the sun. I drew in a deep breath and enjoyed every moment of it. To make it perfect, I spotted two dolphins not too far from me. They were chasing fish and making big splashes in the water. I could have stayed like this all day, just surfing and watching nature, but unfortunately, I had to get out and get to work before nine.

I caught one last wave and rode it to the beach, feeling the wind in my face and the thrill of the ride. I usually rode shorter boards, but on small-wave days like this, I enjoyed longboarding. I practiced my cross-steps and made it almost to the tip of the board before I reached the beach. As I came out of the water, I grabbed my board, then turned around and took one last glance at the beautiful scenery, as if to greet the ocean and say thanks before I ran back up and into the shower.

Surfing always made me feel cheerful, and I was still singing when I arrived at the station. A note on my desk told me the medical examiner's office was done with the initial autopsy. I peeked into Weasel's office and let her know where I was going, then grabbed one of the department's cars and drove to Rockledge on the mainland.

The county had recently gotten a new District Medical Examiner, appointed by the Governor, and I hadn't had a chance to meet him yet. It was very rare we needed their help. It was mostly when tourists committed suicide by jumping off cruise ships and ended washed up on our beaches. Or after bar fights when someone was stabbed. I had liked the former District Medical Examiner, Dr. Parker, but unfortunately, he had retired three months ago and they had to appoint a new one.

I parked in front of the office and walked up. I had put on a hoodie. The temperature today would stay in the high sixties, and I found it to be quite chilly. The sun would probably warm up during the day and make it nice, but for now, it felt good wearing a sweater. In January, you never knew what you'd get. It could go from the low sixties and windy out of the North to the low to mid-eighties in a day or two.

"Jack Ryder. I'm here to see Dr. Díez," I said to the secretary behind the counter, while reading the last name from my note.

The secretary smiled. "One moment, please."

I sat down and found my phone. I started going through my emails and answering as many as possible before a door finally opened and someone stepped out.

"Mr. Ryder?" a voice said.

I stood up. In front of me stood a woman in her mid-forties wearing a white coat. Her thick dark brown hair was gathered in a bun on the back of her head. She was short and slightly overweight. Her brown eyes stared at me.

"Mr. Ryder?" she repeated, and reached out her hand. I grabbed it. "I'm Dr. Díez, District Medical Examiner. Shall we take a look?"

17

January 2015

W e walked down a flight of stairs and entered the autopsy suite.

"So, I guess a welcome is in order, Dr. Díez," I said.

She turned her head and smiled "Thank you, Officer. And you can call me Yamilla."

"Yamilla? That sounds Spanish?"

She walked to a table and put on plastic gloves and a mask. I did the same.

"Cuban," she said. "But I was born in Tampa. My father escaped as a child, just before it was too late."

"So, your mother is American?" I asked, as we walked towards the steel table where the covered body was.

Yamilla grabbed the white blanket and lifted it. "Yes and no. She was born on American soil, but has Cuban roots too. Both her parents are Cuban. We have a way of finding each other. Only she's second generation, and like me, she has never been to Cuba." She paused and glanced down. Then she pulled the blanket off.

I swallowed hard at the sight of Laura Bennett once again. Next to her, on another table, lay the cut off parts. Yamilla took in a deep breath.

"We don't see many of these kinds around here."

"We sure don't," I said, and looked closely at the body. "So, what can you tell me about her?"

"She was strangled to death. But not with his hands or anything tied around her neck. You see, there are no marks on her throat. "The Petechiae under her eyelids is a sign of strangulation. He didn't use his hands."

"He's a gentle killer," I said. I looked at the mouth. "There is no sign of aggression. No anger. Any marks under her upper lips?"

Yamilla smiled. "Someone has seen this before," she said. She grabbed the upper lip and lifted it. "As you can see, she has marks here. Her lip was pressed against her teeth, leaving the marks. But there is nothing on the outside to indicate anything was pressed against her lips."

"A pillow," I said. "Leaves no marks."

"Exactly. The killer went to great lengths to not leave any trace."

I leaned in over Laura Bennett's face and studied it closer. "Or, maybe he didn't want to bruise her. He cares about her body, not about her."

"That could be a theory," Yamilla said.

"Anything else? A time of death?" I asked.

Yamilla looked at me from above her mask. "Between one-thirty and two in the morning."

I wrote it on my notepad, thinking that eliminated Travis Connor, who had been seen at the Beach Shack from ten-twenty till it closed at two. The bartender told me he was positive the guy had stayed there till two, since he had trouble getting him to leave.

"Anything else?"

Yamilla paused. There was something.

"She was washed."

"Yes. We determined on the scene that she had been in the shower," I said. "There were still water drops and dirt on the sides of the bathtub. We figured she had been in the shower when the killer surprised her. That's why I'm quite surprised at the time of death. I was certain it had been in the morning

63

hours. I was sure she had gotten out of bed, then was taking a shower when the killer came in."

"No," Yamilla said. "She was washed after death occurred. She was washed with bleach. There is nothing on her body. It's completely clean. No fingerprints. No DNA. Not even a drop of sweat, which there would be if she struggled for her life during strangulation. Her body would have released noradrenaline, a hormone closely related to adrenaline. Yet, I find no trace of anything on her. It has all been washed away."

18

January 2015

I said goodbye to Dr. Yamilla Díez and hit the road again. Across the first bridge that took me to Merritt Island, the island between my beloved Cocoa Beach and the mainland, I couldn't help thinking about this new information. The killer had washed Laura Bennett's body after he strangled her. Who did that? Who washed her with bleach just before starting to cut her up? Was it some kind of weird ritual? Was it to get rid of DNA? Bleach was known to get rid of DNA. Bleach contained sodium hypochlorite, an extremely corrosive chemical that could break the hydrogen bonds between DNA base pairs and degrade a DNA sample. In fact, bleach was so effective that crime labs used it to clean workspaces so that old samples didn't contaminate fresh evidence.

A picture of the killer had started to shape in my mind. The picture of a guy who took his time with his victim. A killer who enjoyed what he did and wanted the moment to last. He was also very controlled. He made no mistakes. This was no ordinary guy. On top of it, he was gentle with the victim's body.

I passed the second bridge and drove into Cocoa Beach shortly after. Tourists and snowbirds were on the roads everywhere, not knowing where to go, cruising down A1A, slowing the traffic down.

At a meeting at the station, I told everyone what I had learned at the medical examiner's office. They didn't seem to buy into my idea of him being a gentle killer much, especially not Weasel, who looked skeptically at me from her seat at the end of the table.

"I still say we take a closer look at the husband. He's the one with the best motive. It was the wife's money. He's getting everything. She was about to leave him. They lost a child, and he blames her for it. Lots of reasons to finish her off in an angry tantrum while drunk, then pretend to pass out."

"But he doesn't remember anything," Joel Hall said. "When we got to the house and talked to him, he was completely out of it. Hardly knew who he was, let alone what had happened the night before."

"How is the guy doing?" Weasel asked. "Can we interrogate him soon?"

"I was with him last night, Marty took the morning shift," Jim Moore said. "I left the hospital at four in the morning, then slept till nine. Brandon Bennett was completely knocked out all the time I was there. But I can go call Marty and see if there is any news."

"Do that," I said.

Jim left the table with his phone in hand. I looked at the others.

"We have to think about who else might have a motive besides the husband," I said. "He might be telling the truth."

The Weasel snorted. "It's him. I just know it is. I can smell it. He's bad news. Besides, there's no sign of breaking and entering on the house. Whoever did this knew Laura Bennett."

"Being bad news doesn't make you a killer," I said.

"True," Weasel said. But she didn't mean it.

"We need to look in other directions as well," I said. "I've ruled out the neighbor who lives down the street, Travis Connor, since he has an alibi, and as far as we know, he was the only one who visited the house on the night of the killing. But there might have been others. He left pretty early. There could have been someone else. Joel, have the other neighbors said anything useful?"

Joel shook his head with a sigh. "Not really. I mean, Mrs. Jeffries told us she saw Mrs. Bennett smoking on the porch at eleven, but that's about it. No one has seen anyone else on the street. But, I'm not done. I still have a couple of houses left on the street that I haven't talked to, since they weren't home."

"You'll continue that today. There might be someone sitting on important information that they don't think is useful," Weasel said.

Joel Hall shrugged. "Sure. But it is a fairly quiet street, and on a Sunday night, most of the people were in bed early."

Weasel smacked her hand on the table. "Come on. This can't be it, people. Someone must have seen something. At least they must have heard her scream. Ask if anyone heard any screams between one and two in the morning."

"There was loud music coming from the Bennett's house," Joel Hall said. "It could have drowned out any screams. Besides, people are so used to hearing them quarrel."

"Plus, she was strangled by a pillow," I said. "She probably couldn't scream."

Weasel growled and leaned back in her chair with a *mommy isn't happy* look on her face.

"I'll ask around anyway," Joel Hall said, to smooth things out.

At the same time, the door opened, and Jim Moore stepped in. "He's awake," he said. "Brandon Bennett is awake."

19

January 2015

"I don't remember anything. I swear. I really don't."

Brandon Bennett was sitting up in his bed at Cape Canaveral Hospital. Marty had taken his son, Ben, and the dog to the cafeteria to get a hot cocoa at my suggestion, while I spoke to the dad. The dog had been allowed to stay overnight, given the circumstances. Everyone felt bad for Ben and wanted him to feel safe. I talked to the doctor before entering the room, and he confirmed that Brandon Bennett had been drugged with Rohypnol, or a Roofie, as it was also called. The date-rape drug. That was why he had been so out of it and why he had been slipping in and out of consciousness for the past twenty-four hours. I had called Yamilla at the medical examiner's office and she told me they had already checked Laura Bennett's blood, and there were no signs of any drugs. Lots of alcohol, but no other drugs. In other words, it was only Brandon Bennett who had been drugged. That told me the killer just wanted to get rid of Brandon, and that Laura had been his real target. That was my theory.

I got up and walked to the window of the third floor. The hospital was situated on a small peninsula and had water on three sides of it. Brandon Bennett's room had views over the

Banana River, with Cape Canaveral's huge cruise ships on the horizon waiting to take off later in the day.

"You gotta help me out a little, here, Brandon," I said. "Your wife turns up killed in your bedroom after a night you and she had been drinking heavily. We learn from neighbors and friends that you often fight loudly and violently, especially since the death of your child. People tell me you blame her for it. With her death, you're going to inherit a lot of money. You like to gamble. Convince me that you didn't kill her."

I turned and looked at his face. He was pale and looked ill. He threw out his hands. "I…I don't know what else to say."

I rubbed my forehead, then stared at him, scrutinizing him. Was he a brilliant liar? Or was he telling the truth? He didn't seem to be that bad guy everyone else was so busy making him out to be.

"Did you do it?" I asked. Mostly because I had to. I knew what answer he would give me.

Brandon Bennett looked appalled. "Of course not. Are you kidding me? I loved Laura. I adored her. If she was here, she could tell you. I gave her flowers every week. Ask the local florist. Every freaking Wednesday I had her send my wife flowers. I loved everything about her. I know I was never the model husband or father. I have a problem. I'll admit to that. I drink and I gamble. And I hate myself for that. Believe me. It is destroying me and my marriage."

His voice cracked as he spoke. It made him sound sincere. I cursed it. I really wanted him to be guilty. I wanted him to be the bad news Gabrielle Phillips had talked about. But when I looked at him, that wasn't what I saw. Tears were piling up in his eyes now as he looked at me. His body was shaking from the restraint of holding them back.

He was truly sad that his wife was gone.

"I have no idea how to do this on my own," he said. A tear escaped the corner of his eye and rolled across his cheek.

I handed him a tissue.

"What about Ben? How is he going to get by without his mother?" he asked, choking up.

"All right," I said and nodded. "Let's say I believe you. How much do you remember? Let's start with Sunday evening. What did you do?"

Brandon Bennett sniffled and wiped his nose. "We ordered pizza. Then Laura put Ben to bed. We had a couple of drinks. It was sort of an anniversary for us."

"What were you celebrating?" I asked.

"Not celebrating. Drowning our sorrows while trying to forget. It was a year since our daughter died."

I noted it on my notepad while biting my lip. I couldn't even imagine how devastating it had to be to lose a child. Thinking of any of my three kids, it hurt inside to imagine being without them.

"Okay, so you were drinking. What else?"

Brandon Bennett looked like he was thinking. "It's all a little blurry, but I believe Travis came over and had a drink or two," he said. "He didn't stay long, though. He wanted to hit the Beach Shack when they opened. I guess we weren't such great company either. We were pretty depressed. When he left, we started fighting, as we always did when we had a little too much to drink."

"What were you fighting about?" I asked, studying his face for reactions to what he was saying.

"I actually don't remember," he said. "Probably what we always fight about."

"And what is that?" I asked.

"My gambling. It always starts with her telling me I gamble too much, and that it's her money I'm using. Then, I blame her for losing our child, and after that, there's no turning back."

"I can imagine there isn't," I said with a sigh. I remembered the things Arianna and I could say to one another during a fight. It wasn't pretty. Why did couples do this to one another?

"What else do you remember?"

He shrugged. "That's it. We fought and then we went to bed."

I looked at him with dissatisfaction. "And you can't remember what time you went to bed, I take it?"

He shook his head. "No."

"Did anyone else come over during the night?"

"I…I…"

"You don't remember," I said, and wrote it down.

"There might have been someone else. It's all very blurry."

"So, what else do you remember? Do you remember waking up and the police coming to the house?" I asked.

He shook his head again. "I don't. I remember drinking and fighting, and then waking up here in the hospital a couple of hours ago, and being told what happened."

"That's all?" I asked.

"Yes. I'm sorry, Officer. I seem to have lost a big part of my memory. The doctor told me it was the drug. Mixed with alcohol, it messes with one's memory completely. Again, I'm sorry. I really want to help."

I put my pen away and was ready to leave. "Well, Mr. Bennett. The doctor told me you'll be able to take your son home later today. Don't leave town, all right? We're not done here."

Brandon Bennett shook his head. "I have no intention of doing that. I want this guy as bad as you do, Officer."

"I'm glad. But for now, make sure you take care of your son. He needs you more than ever."

"I will. Thank you, Officer."

I was walking towards the door, when Brandon Bennett suddenly stopped me.

"Wait. There was something." Brandon Bennett looked pensive. "There was someone there. Was it…I think it was."

"Who?"

"Peter," he said, looking directly at me. "Peter stopped by right before midnight. He was angry."

I found my notepad and my pen. Finally, something I could work with.

"Who is Peter?"

"That's her brother. Her older brother."

"The writer's son? Who grew up in her biological father's house?"

Brandon's face cleared up. "Yes. He was the youngest of the three, and the only one we had any contact with."

20

September 1984

"I'm pregnant and it's yours."

Annie spoke with a quivering voice. She stood in front of Tim in the library, where she had finally found him and approached him. He hadn't responded to her phone calls or her letters, nor had he stopped to talk with her when she approached him on campus. Finally, she had found him sitting in the reading chairs at the library with his friends. It had taken all of her courage to approach him like this, but it had to be done. It was the only way she could get him to listen. At first, she had asked him to step outside with her, told him she had something important and very private to tell him, but he had refused. Laughed to her face and refused.

Now, his face froze in a smile and all his friends stared at her.

"What?" he asked.

"You heard me."

He lifted his pointer. "No, no. You have it all wrong, little missy."

"No, I don't," she said. "It's yours. I'm five months pregnant."

Tim's friends stared at him, waiting for his response. So did Annie. Her legs were shaking, threatening to give in to the rest of her body. She had never been this nervous in her life.

Tim stared at her with big eyes, then shook his head. "I'm not falling for that. Who told you to say this, huh? Was it Chris, huh? Ha ha, Chris. Very funny. You can stop it now."

"It's not a joke," she said. "It happened that night by the lake."

Tim shook his head. "I haven't the faintest idea what you're talking about. I think you've got the wrong person."

Annie stepped forward. "You need to marry me."

The reading room went completely silent. No one was tapping their fingers, no one clearing their throat or coughing. And no one was reading anymore. All eyes were on them.

Tim withered in his leather chair. He looked at her with serious eyes. She could see the fear in them. The fear of his life, as he knew it, being over. Of the anger of his parents. The fear of having to live with someone for the rest of his life that he didn't love or even care for.

Those few minutes of indecision finally mounted into a big smile, followed by loud laughter.

"Marry you? Ha! That's a good one. Very funny. Now get out of here before I make you."

"Tim, it's the right thing to do. For the child's sake. For my sake. My parents are going to renounce me. Without them, I have no money, I have nothing. This child will grow up in the gutter."

Tim scoffed. "What do I care? Don't have the child, then. It's not my child anyway. I wouldn't touch that ugly body of yours, even if you paid me to."

Tim's friends laughed.

Annie felt her anger rise. Tears piled up in her eyes. "It is yours."

He leaned over in his chair. "How do you know?"

"Because I haven't been with anyone else but you…ever." She knew it wasn't the entire truth. They both knew. His friends had been there too that night. They had all raped her. It could be any of them. As they stared into each other's eyes in a power struggle, they both knew she would never have a paternity test taken because that meant she would have to admit to having been with multiple men on that night. It was simply too shameful for her.

"Get out of here," Tim yelled. His face showed real anger now. His nostrils were flaring.

Tears rolling across her cheeks, Annie backed up, frightened of what Tim and his friends might do to her if she stayed. When she reached the front door, she opened it and ran. She ran across campus as fast as she could, the sound of the blood rushing through her veins drowning out everything else. When she couldn't run anymore, she threw herself on the grass, crying heavily, covering her eyes with her hands. Her stomach was in her way constantly now, and she loathed it more than ever. She loathed what had happened to her, and worst of all, she loathed this baby and what it was going to do to her life. Still, she couldn't kill it. She could never do *that*.

"What is to become of me?" she cried out, staring at the stars in the sky, wondering if there was a God and whether he could even hear her. It seemed like he didn't these days.

"I'll take care of you," a voice said.

Annie turned her head with a small gasp and stared into the eyes of Victor. Victor was the campus' biggest nerd. He was strange and awkward and all wrong. But he had always had a thing for Annie. Growing up in the same town and going to the same schools, he had adored her ever since he laid eyes on her for the first time in preschool. And he followed her everywhere. Even to the same college. But Annie couldn't stand the guy. He was always clinging to her in high school, making life miserable for her because none of the cool kids wanted to hang out with her because of him. God, how she had hated him for many years. Even the way he smelled, or the way he said hi and pressed his glasses back on his forehead when he did. The way he dressed, the way his hair was always greasy and falling onto his forehead. In college, she had managed to keep him at a distance, but he still seemed to be everywhere she went.

Had he followed her here? Had he heard what she had told Tim?

He reached out his hand towards her.

"I was in the library. I heard everything," he said. "I'll take care of you. That bastard doesn't deserve you. I'll marry you."

21

January 2015

Peter Walker lived in a modest two-bedroom condo in Cape Canaveral. I had called in advance and told him I would stop by to make sure he was home. He had the daytime off, he told me when he opened the door and let me in.

"Where do you work?" I asked, as I closed the door behind me.

The condo was a mess. Dogs and cats roamed the living room and were fighting as I entered. It smelled like a pet store.

"At Ron Jon's."

Ron Jon is the biggest surf store in the world, located in Cocoa Beach. It started as a surf shop, but had now evolved into just as much of a souvenir shop for tourists who come to see the store that is open twenty-four hours a day. It has become a landmark for the town and something people talk about. Tourists buy T-shirts with Ron Jon's logo on them and walk around town wearing them. Stickers with their logos are on many of the cars, since they come with every purchase you make. It is a big and booming business, but also causes a struggle for the smaller surf shops around town. I never buy anything in there, since I have all my boards shaped by a local shaper to fit me perfectly. The shop is good for the town and the tourist industry, and they have nice boards, but to be honest, I prefer supporting the smaller local places. That's just the way I am.

"I work the nightshift," he continued, as I sat down on his couch.

"That's a bummer," I said, and took out my notepad and threw it on the table, then found my pen in my pocket.

"So, what can I do for you, Officer?" he asked. "I understood it was about my sister, Laura?"

I nodded, then flipped to a blank page in my pad. "Yes. Your sister Laura. As you probably know by now, she was found killed yesterday morning at her house in Snug Harbor."

Peter sat down as well. "Yes. I heard. Any news about what happened to her?"

I exhaled. "That depends. How well do you know her?"

He shook his head. "She was only my half-sister. I didn't know she existed until my father died."

"So, it's safe to say not very well?" I asked.

"I hardly knew her at all, to be frank," he said. "Even after we knew who she was, I never had the urge to get to know her, if you know what I mean. None of us wanted to know her."

"Why is that? Because she took your inheritance?"

Peter leaned back in his recliner. "Well, yes. Can you blame me? Can you blame us for not wanting her in our lives? She took everything. Came from out of nowhere and took it all. Now, I have to live like this, and I have to work nights at a job I hate. I could have been living the life. I could have been rich."

"To be fair, it was your father's money. He could have given it to a charity. He was entitled to do with the money as he pleased, don't you think? Laura didn't know her real dad growing up. Don't you think it's fair she got a little compensation for being lied to her entire life? After all, you and your sisters had everything growing up, didn't you? She needed that fatherly love, from her real father," I said, deliberately provoking him.

Peter was moving in his seat. What I said struck a chord.

"We had everything, you say? How about, we had nothing? We lived with a father who was never there. We grew up in a house with a father who was never home, and even if he was present, he wasn't there mentally. He would stay in his office and write all his stupid stories about characters that he loved way more than he ever loved any of us. After our mother died, he kept dragging new and younger models home with him from book tours, or wherever he went. They would stay at the house for months and hang by the pool, drinking margaritas at ten in the morning, then he would throw them out once he was tired of them. We never saw him or felt his fatherly love either. None of us did. So, don't come and say she was the one who needed the money the most. At least she grew up in a house with a mother and father that loved her. We didn't. Our dad didn't care about us at all."

Peter was spitting while he talked. I could tell I had upset him.

"So, it is fair to say you're pretty pissed at Laura, right? You and your sisters are all pretty angry with her?"

Peter touched his hair and leaned back. He finally understood why I had come. He calmed down. "I didn't kill her," he said.

"That didn't sound convincing at all," I said.

"Well, it's the truth."

"You were seen in the house," I said. "Someone saw you there on the night she was killed."

Peter exhaled deeply. "I guess I knew you would somehow figure out I was there," he said. "Well, okay. I was there. But I didn't kill her."

"Convince me. Tell me you have an alibi for where you were between one and two in the morning," I said.

Peter swallowed hard. "I...I can't. I was here. I was at home. I went to Laura's house around eleven-thirty, but came back here at one."

"Why did you go to the house? Why were you there if it wasn't to kill her for taking your birthright?"

Peter thought for a long time. I could tell he was debating within himself. I saw that exact same expression on people's faces constantly. He was definitely hiding something.

"I went to ask for money," he almost whispered.

"What was that? Money? Why would she give you money?"

"She gave me money now and then. To help me out."

I leaned back, feeling baffled. "Why? Why would she give you money if you didn't know each other very well?"

He shrugged. He reached over the table, grabbed a cigarette, and lit it. His hands were shaking. He was very nervous.

"I guess she was trying to be nice to me. I am, after all, her brother." He blew smoke in my face. I hated that smell.

"So, you mean to tell me you came to her house right before midnight to get some money that she now and then gave to you as a gift?"

Peter inhaled again. "Yes," he said with a small smirk.

"Do you find this funny?" I asked.

He shrugged. "Not really."

"So, she gave you money now and then. How much are we talking about?" I asked to get the conversation moving. I was already late to pick up Abigail and Austin. I had promised them I'd do it myself today. On top of that, I was starving. I hadn't had any lunch. Not eating made me grumpy.

"A couple of thousand. Once she gave me twenty."

"Twenty thousand dollars. She's a nice sister, huh? Especially for someone you don't know very well or care for."

"She was all right. Guess she felt bad for me."

"What about the others?" I asked.

"What about them?" he said indifferently.

He was starting to annoy me. He thought he was real clever now, trying to pretend he didn't care. He knew I didn't have any evidence to bring him up on yet. It was hardly enough just to have visited the house on the night of the murder.

"Did they receive money like you did? Did Laura give them generous gifts as well?"

Peter shook his head. "I have no idea."

"I guess you don't know them very well either, huh?" I said and got up. I was tired of talking to this guy. It was getting me nowhere. I threw my card on the table before I left.

"Call me in case you remember anything. And don't leave town."

22

January 2015

R honda Harris glanced out the window one last time. The yellow police tape across the street was swaying in the wind. Two police cars were still parked outside in the front yard. A small minivan was parked in the driveway. She knew it belonged to the medical examiner's office. They were taking samples, looking for fingerprints, searching the house for anything that could bring them closer to the killer. Rhonda knew the procedure. She had studied them and researched the police's work for years. She had taken classes; she had been on patrol with the police, visited the medical examiner's office, and read tons of books about forensic evidence. Yes, Rhonda Harris was a true expert when it came to police work, and that was what scared her.

She knew they would eventually come for her. She knew it was a matter of days, maybe hours, before they would knock on her front door and confront her.

It was a beautiful day out. As beautiful as they came in January in Cocoa Beach. She had always enjoyed winter far more than she did summer, she thought to herself. She loved the beach at this time of year and would take long walks there. Especially on cooler windier days like this one, when it was nice out, but a little too chilly to actually lie on the beach. Those were the days when the snowbirds and tourists went to the outlets and parks in Orlando or visited Ron Jon's surf shop to get their T-shirts and key chains. Those were the days when she would have the beach all to herself.

Rhonda looked at the cat on her desk next to her computer. He liked to sleep right next to her picture of her daughter and her husband, who lived up in New York now.

What will they think? What will they think of me when they find out what I've done?

The cat stretched and a pen fell to the floor. It rolled across the wooden floor and stopped close to Rhonda's feet. She picked it up. Then she chuckled. The pen was one she had bought when visiting Hemingway's house in the Keys ten years ago.

Why did you do it, Rhonda? Why did you have to do that stupid thing?

Rhonda shivered and forced herself to think about her daughter. She had found all the old photos and gone through them all morning, while tears streamed from her eyes. Pictures of Kate when she was just a child, then of the grandchildren from just a few years ago. So many good memories, so much love.

We had a good run, didn't we? We had fun.

Rhonda sniffled again and wiped her nose on a tissue. Then, she looked at a picture of her belated husband. John had been everything to her.

"I'm sorry for this, John," she whispered. "I never meant for it to go this far. Life was hard after you left. I had nothing. This was my way out. But it ran off with me. I got greedy, I guess. I'm sorry."

She looked at her husband and thought he looked back at her with contempt.

Will they ever forgive me? They're all gonna be angry, aren't they? They'll resent me for this.

The cat purred in his sleep. Rhonda petted his head gently, wondering what was to become of him.

"Hopefully, Kate and the kids will take you to New York

with them once all this is over," she said. "You'll like it there. Take good care of the kids for me, will you?"

Rhonda touched the cat's fur again and stroked it gently. The cat purred and rolled to the side. He was still sleeping.

How wonderful it must be to be a cat. Just sleep through everything. Not a care in the world.

She had filled his bowls with water and food, in case it was a long time before they came. It probably wasn't necessary, since they were just across the street and would come quickly when they heard the noise. She put the letter by John's picture on her desk. She leaned over and kissed the cat, before opening the drawer and pulling out the gun.

"I sure hope I'll see you on the other side, John," she whispered through tears.

Without giving herself even a second to think about it twice, she put the cold gun against her temple and pulled the trigger.

23

January 2015

bigail and Austin were in the front office when I arrived at the school. They were sitting in the chairs looking angrily at me when I entered through the glass doors.

"I'm so, so sorry," I said, feeling awful. "I lost track of time."

"That's okay, Jack," Elaine said from behind the counter. She smiled. "Everybody is late from time to time."

I turned and looked at the two angry faces. They got up, Abigail with a deep annoyed sigh. They walked to the car, giving me the cold shoulder.

"Guys, I said I was sorry," I said.

"You promised you would be on time. School's out at two-thirty, not three-thirty, Dad," Abigail growled reproachfully.

"I said I was sorry," I repeated, and started the car. I turned to check that they both had their seatbelts on before I backed out of the parking lot.

"Where were you anyway?" Austin asked.

"I had to talk to this guy," I said.

"Is he a murderer?" Austin asked with excitement.

"Well…No one is guilty until we prove otherwise, but he did have my interest," I said diplomatically. Truth was, I had a bad feeling about Peter Walker. He was definitely hiding something. I just had no idea what it was. He had been at the scene of the crime shortly before she was killed. He had a motive. A good one. And he had no alibi for where he was at the time of death.

"Wow," Austin exclaimed. "That's so cool. Are you going to lock him away?"

I loved that Austin thought my job was so interesting. It was one of the few things that could get him really excited.

"Maybe," I said, and hit A1A towards my parents' motel. "But you know that first we have to find enough evidence, and so far, we don't have much on this guy."

"But he is your suspect, right?"

"He is one of them, yes."

"Cool."

I parked the car in the lot in front of my parents' motel, grabbed the kids' backpacks, and walked inside. I had texted Emily and told her to come here after school. She went to Cocoa Beach High and had band-practice after school today.

Abigail hadn't uttered a word since the school. I put my arm around her and pulled her closer.

"So, how was your day?" I asked.

She shrugged. "Good. Until you forgot about us."

Abigail was always the one I had to work on longer to get her to forgive me. Austin forgot right away when I messed up, but not Abigail.

"I didn't forget you. I was just a little late. And I did say I was sorry. Can you forgive me?"

She stopped and looked into my eyes. She was so strong, I couldn't believe it. At her age. So determined, so willed at heart. She was the type who could amount to something if she set her heart on it. She was going to rule the world one day. Maybe be president. For now, she ruled my heart, and that was more than enough.

"Okay, Dad." She petted me on my arm. "I know you do your best. Just don't do it again. Have Grandma pick us up instead, okay?"

"That's a promise. Now, let's go see if Grandma has something we can eat. I'm starving," I said, and grabbed her hand in mine. Austin had already disappeared into the back.

"Me too," Abigail said. "But, just between you and me, I really don't like the snacks Grandma has."

"Me either," I whispered, thinking of the dry crackers I had the last time I was there in the afternoon. I was hoping she would make me a burger or a fish sandwich. Maybe a crab cake. She was very good at those.

"But, don't tell her," Abigail said. "She'll get sad."

"Oh, and we don't want that, do we?"

"Nope."

24

January 2015

"I S THAT YOU, SON?"

The old man was sitting in the darkness of the living room when the Snakecharmer entered through the front door. He had parked his wheelchair in the corner and the Snakecharmer wondered how long he had been sitting there.

The blind old bat.

"Grandpa!"

The old man smiled as his grandson threw himself in his arms. "It is you," he said with an exhale.

"Yeah, Dad. It's us," the Snakecharmer said. "Who else would it be? Are you expecting company?"

"No," the old man said, chuckling. "Who would want to visit an old blind fool like me?"

"We bought cake," the Snakecharmer said, and placed a grocery bag on the table. He turned on the light in the room. "And beer."

The Snakecharmer opened one for himself, then threw his body on the couch while the boy went into his room. The house was one of those from the fifties, with three bedrooms and two old baths, across the street from the beach, and looked like a bungalow. It was small, but it fit the three of them perfectly.

"Everything all right, Son?" his dad asked.

The Snakecharmer placed a beer in his hand. His dad chuckled again. "Ah, the little things. It's funny how you learn to appreciate them when you don't have much. Like a cold beer on a warm day." He lifted the beer and sipped it. He made a satisfied sound. The area where his eyes used to be was completely disfigured. They had removed his eyes, since there was nothing left from when the acid hit. The skin on his face looked like it was melted. Most people who looked at him felt bad, or discomfort, but not the Snakecharmer. The Snakecharmer liked to stare at his father's disfigured face, and would do so for a long time every now and then. And he was doing so now while drinking his beer. Staring and drinking, while the anger inside of him arose, the anger towards those bitches still out there that he had to rid the world of.

"Cake, you said?" the old man asked.

The Snakecharmer laughed. His dad loved cake. Cake and beer. A strange combination for many people, but not for his father.

"I'll get us some plates," the Snakecharmer said.

"Don't forget to feed the snakes," the old man said, and sipped his beer again. "They seem hungry. Been making a lot of noise today."

The Snakecharmer looked at the glass cage in the corner. He approached it and stared at Mango, his favorite snake. A sixteen-foot Burmese python. One of those that could swallow a child, or that you heard of eating its owner if it wasn't fed. He loved that snake, even though he never took it on the road with him. The snakes he used for that were two Coral snakes that he kept in the cage next to the python. They ate mostly insects and were easy to control, as long as they were fed. Drago and Django were their names.

"I won't," the Snakecharmer said, and stared at the python sleeping on its branch. "I stopped by the pet store on my way here and bought some."

The Snakecharmer had loved snakes ever since he was a small child. He used to catch them and play with them. He would let them bite his hands and arms and look at the blood as it dripped onto the ground. It was mostly black racers that he played with, but he also caught rattlesnakes and skinned them and put their skins up on the wall of his room.

"How about that cake?" his dad asked.

The Snakecharmer chuckled. His eyes still didn't leave the python. He couldn't stop staring at it. Snakes fascinated him. The way they moved so quietly. Then he pulled out two mice in a small container. He caught one by the tail, lifted it above the tank, lifted the lid, and dropped it inside. Then, he waited. Waited with his eyes fixated on the snake who was now waking up and moving towards the mouse. He stared at the mouse, while sensing its fear as it faced the mighty snake. When the snake made his move so fast the mouse hardly realized what happened, and swallowed the mouse in one bite, he laughed.

It was that easy being the predator.

25

January 2015

My mom made a ton of crab cakes for me, and I ate till my stomach hurt. I washed it all down with a sweetened iced tea, homemade naturally. We sat on the deck at the beach and watched the waves while eating. Abigail grabbed a couple of dry crackers and ate them, while smiling.

She was getting to be quite the actress.

After eating, the kids wanted to run down to the beach and fly a kite. I found an old one in the closet inside my parents' living quarters at the very end of the building. While walking along the doors to the many rooms, I thought about how much I loved this place. At first, when my parents had told me their dream of investing in a small motel on the beach, I thought it was the stupidest idea ever. I couldn't believe they would rather spend their pension on this, instead of enjoying the money and relaxing like they were supposed to when growing old.

But not my parents. No, they always had to have something to do. It had always been like that. My mother loved to cook and take care of others, while my dad loved to have guests and be with people. He talked to everyone who arrived at the motel, and some of them ended up becoming their friends. People returned because of him. He created such a warm atmosphere, people were willing to accept old buildings and bad plumbing. The rooms were nicely decorated, my mom had made sure of that. She had a great flair for decorating and made sure all the rooms looked nice and were clean. She didn't clean them herself, but had Jennifer, a small nice Asian woman to take care of it.

Jennifer was like family to all of us, and often joined us for dinner. Her daughter lived in Daytona Beach with her husband, and other than that, Jennifer didn't have anyone around here. We didn't mind being her family.

"You found one!" Austin exclaimed, excited when he saw the kite in my hand as I approached the beach. I took off my shoes and dug my toes into the sand. It felt good. I was a beach boy and never liked to cramp my feet into socks and shoes much. But I had to at work. Even though I preferred to be barefoot or wear flip-flops.

"Yes. Let's put it up," I said, and looked at the trees to determine the wind's direction. I was quite the weather-geek, and at my place at the condo I rented, I had put up a weather station in one of the trees, hoping no one would complain about it. I followed the winds and temperatures closely. The wind was still blowing out of the north. It was supposed to shift later in the day, I had seen in my weather app. I was looking forward to that. If the wind was off-shore all night, it would make perfect conditions for surfing in the morning. And the swell was supposed to build in the coming days, so it could turn out to be epic.

"What do I do, Dad?" Austin asked, as I handed him the kite.

"Let me show you."

I had barely finished my sentence before the phone rang in my pocket. At first, I thought about letting it ring. This was my time with the kids, but then I remembered it might be about the case. When working a big case like this, I couldn't just fall off the surface of the earth.

"One second," I said, and grabbed the phone in my pocket.

"Ryder."

It was Weasel's raspy voice.

"We have another one."

I swallowed hard. "Say what again?"

"Another dead body on West Bay Drive. You won't believe it. It's right across the street from the Bennetts' house."

26

October 1984

I t was a small wedding. Just for the family. Annie's
mother wanted it to be that way, since it was obvious to
everyone why they were getting married.

Annie never told her family that Victor wasn't the father
of the child she was carrying. There was no need to. It would
only upset them. Besides, Victor wanted to be the father; he
wanted everyone to think he was the father, so they both
pretended and kept smiling.

"Victor is such a nice guy," Annie's mother told her after
the ceremony, when they were eating appetizers from their
plates in the backyard of Victor's childhood home, where his
parents insisted the ceremony be held.

They didn't seem as fond of Annie as Victor was. Especially not the circumstances under which the marriage had
been arranged.

"And he has money," Annie's Aunt Anita whispered and
swallowed one of the salmon appetizers. "Nice score. So what
if he isn't among the handsomest of men? At least he's
loaded."

Annie couldn't stand hearing her mom and aunt go on
about Victor and how perfect he was. As a matter of fact, she
had a hard time going through with this wedding at all. The

baby was growing rapidly inside of her, and it was very visible now. Victor's mother couldn't stop staring at it in contempt. Annie felt that her white dress was too tight. She felt like she was about to suffocate. And, worst of all, she couldn't stand what was ahead of her. She couldn't stand the thought of having to spend the rest of her life with that geek, Victor, and having a child when she wasn't sure who the father was.

At least you don't have to go through it alone. At least he cares for you. At least he'll make sure you never need anything.

"Are you all right, darling?" Victor whispered, as he rescued her from her mother and aunt. He took her hand and pulled her away from them. They took a stroll in the garden. It felt good to get away from the people and the pretending. Behind the estate was a small park. They found a bench and sat down. Annie didn't care if her white dress got dirty, but could hear her mother's voice tell her to never sit on a dirty bench wearing white. Would that voice ever leave her head? Would she ever be free from her parents?

Part of her couldn't stand the future she had in front of her. Looking at Victor, it felt like she had just married her parents. It was nothing like she had planned. Her life wasn't going to turn out anything like she had planned on those lonely nights in her bedroom as a child.

"You look pale." He kissed her on the cheek.

The kiss made her shiver in disgust. She lifted her eyes and gazed at him. Then, she forced a smile. Just like she had when he had told her he would marry her and make an honest woman of her. Just like she had done when the priest had told him he could kiss the bride and Victor had lifted the veil. She faked it.

"I'm fine, darling. I'm just really tired. That's all."

Victor smiled calmly. "That's the pregnancy." He put a hand on her belly and felt it. His touch made Annie shiver again. She tried to hide it and lowered her eyes.

"You're probably right. I feel so tired all the time lately.

My doctor says it's normal. And with all the throwing up, it's only natural to be tired."

"You have a life growing inside of you. It's a big thing, darling. You need your rest. Our baby needs his rest."

Annie gasped lightly and looked into Victor's smiling eyes. It was the first time he had mentioned the baby between them as being his. Annie looked into his eyes, wondering if he really meant it or if he was just acting. Was he really capable of forgetting how this baby had come to the world? Would he really be able to consider it to be his? Never once had he asked about the circumstances. All he knew was, Tim had gotten Annie pregnant and wouldn't take responsibility. It was like he didn't even want to know more.

"There you are," Annie's mother chirped and grabbed Annie's hand. "The photographer is here. You two love birds better get back to the party."

Annie looked tiredly at her smiling mother, who was standing slightly tipsy with a glass of bubbling champagne in one hand and Annie's hand in the other.

Oh, my God. She was enjoying this, wasn't she? She was happy to see her daughter marry a guy she didn't love. A guy that could support her. A guy from a good family. A guy with money to secure her for the rest of her life. This was exactly the kind of man her mother had wanted her to marry, wasn't it? Feeling like the dress was getting tighter, she found it harder to breathe; she pulled out her hand from her mother's.

"Is something wrong?" her mother asked.

Victor chuckled and shook his head. "No, Mrs. Greenfield. Everything is perfect, he said. "It's just the pregnancy. It's wearing her out, poor thing." He stroked her cheek gently, while looking at her with compassion.

Annie felt like throwing up.

"Oh my," her mother said and grabbed Annie's arm. She helped her get back to her feet. Then, she stroked Annie's cheek as well. Annie felt like screaming.

"We can't have widdle Annie-bannie get tooo tired-wired, can we now? No, we can't."

27

January 2015

I **left the** kids with my parents, then jumped inside my Jeep and raced to Snug Harbor. Luckily, it was only a three-minute drive from my parents' motel. The medical examiner's van was already parked next to the van from the Sheriff's crime scene unit, an ambulance, and several police cars.

"Hey, Jack," Weasel yelled, as I arrived and parked the car. She seemed tired and her face longer than usual.

"So, what have we got?" I asked, as we walked under the tape and into the house. "Another homicide?"

"It's on the second floor," she said, and we grabbed plastic gloves in the foyer, then walked up the stairs. Through the window on the second floor, I spotted the Bennetts' house that was still blocked by police tape, and wondered if this killer really was so stupid as to strike twice in the same neighborhood.

"Woman, age sixty-seven," Weasel said, as we walked through the hallway and into a big bedroom with bamboo furniture. We stopped at the body on the light carpet. Her face was unrecognizable; blood was sprayed all over the carpet. A gun was lying on the carpet next to her hand.

"Her name was Rhonda Harris," Weasel said.

"Looks like she shot herself?" I asked.

The Weasel nodded. "That's what the ME said."

"Yes, I said that," a voice said behind me.

I turned and spotted Yamilla. She was hard to recognize in all her equipment. I moved and let her get closer to the body.

"I will have to examine her further in my lab, but yes, so far, it's safe to say it was suicide. Shot herself right through the temple."

I got up and looked around. I looked at her computer, her notebooks, and her many books spread all over the floor and tables.

"Looks like she was quite the avid reader," I said.

"Sure does," Weasel said.

"All John Platt books, huh?"

Weasel looked confused. "Well, I hadn't noticed, but I think you might be right. All the open ones are."

I threw a glance out the window at the house across the street.

Weasel rubbed her forehead. "Second death this week in this neighborhood, one of the nicest in town," she sighed. "Gonna be another late nighter for us. If this keeps happening, I'm not going to be so popular around here anymore."

I patted her shoulder while staring at the Bennetts' house. The case had started to haunt me...now more than ever. There was no way these two deaths weren't related somehow.

"What's going on around here?" Weasel asked, wiping her sweaty forehead with a tissue. It was a very moist evening.

"It never used to be like this," she continued. "What do you make of it?"

"Let's just say, I hardly think it's a coincidence that she is a big John Platt fan," I said.

"You think she knew something?" Weasel asked. "You don't think she...she killed Laura?"

I shrugged. "I think she might have known something. Something important. Who was she? What do we know about her?"

"She used to be a reporter for Florida Today, but retired early four years ago," Joel said as he approached us. "Sorry to interrupt, but I just spoke with her daughter up in New York. She's on her way down. Caught a late flight out. Should be here late tonight."

I looked at Joel. He seemed a lot more together than the last time I had seen him. He was still sweating heavily, but we all were.

"Perfect," I said. "Have her come and talk to me tomorrow morning. And I need everything secured from Rhonda Harris' house. Every notebook, her computer, everything she has in those drawers. If she has a knife, I want it checked for blood or Laura Bennett's DNA."

28

January 2015

The waves were crashing on the beach when I woke up the next morning. I had slept with my window open to the balcony. They were luring me in. The sound was intoxicating. They were definitely calling for me.

I felt exhausted when I finally sat up. I didn't arrive to pick up the kids from my parents' place till around nine-thirty the night before. Emily had gone back to the condo by herself, but the twins were fast asleep, so my mother suggested they stay for the night. They had decorated a bedroom for them with bunk beds and SpongeBob posters and everything, and the kids loved sleeping over, so I told her all right and went back to spend the rest of the evening with Emily. We watched a movie together and I made popcorn. I got the feeling she enjoyed it, even though she didn't say so. It was just like back in Miami before the twins had come into our lives. Just Emily and me. I couldn't help looking at her when she didn't see it. I saw so much of her mother in her, more and more every day now. I missed Lisa. She had been the best colleague and friend I had ever had. I was happy I got to see her daughter grow up.

When I woke up at six, I put on my wetsuit, but left the upper part hanging from my waist, grabbed my board, and ran with it across the beach to my parents' motel.

"Daaad!" Austin smiled happily when he saw me. They were sitting on the wooden deck eating waffles. I kissed them both.

"Where were you last night?" Abigail asked. "You never came back."

I sat down next to her and grabbed a waffle for myself. My mother brought me orange juice in a glass. It was freshly squeezed. Nothing beats Florida oranges. "I had to work," I said.

"Did you catch the killer?" Austin asked, excited.

I shook my head and took another bite of my waffle. My mom brought me coffee. "Thank you," I said, and gave her a big kiss on the cheek. "Dad's still sleeping?"

She nodded.

"So, did you?" Austin asked again.

"Nope. Not yet."

The Millers came down the stairs and grabbed the table next to us. I smiled and nodded. My mother brought them breakfast while they discussed Blue Springs State Park, where they were going today.

"We hope to see some manatees," Mrs. Miller said.

"You should be able to," my mother replied, while pouring coffee for them. "At this time of year, there are a lot of them up there at the springs. They like that the water stays the same temperature all year around, you know?"

"So, are you going to catch the killer today?" Austin asked with his mouth full.

I chuckled. "I hope so."

"It's not that easy, Austin," Abigail growled, sounding like the true big sister she was with her fifty-eight seconds. "First, they have to gather all the evidence and talk to a lot of people before they can put him away. It's not all like in the movies."

Austin made a grimace at his sister. She threw a waffle at him.

"Hey, hey," I stopped them. "I won't have you fighting. You hear me? We're family. We need to stick together. Now, did you have a good time with Grandma and Grandpa?"

Austin and Abigail both nodded.

"Good. They will pick you up today from school again. It's early release day, and I have asked them to step in, since I'll be busy with the big case. All right?"

They looked at each other, then cheered.

"Yaay!"

I walked them to the school bus and kissed both of them goodbye as Mrs. Sharon opened the doors to the big yellow bus.

"Now, be good today. Don't get in trouble, all right?" I said.

"You too, Dad," Abigail said, and kissed my nose as I bent down to look into her eyes. "Stay out of trouble."

I laughed and waved as the bus disappeared, then I sprang for my board and threw myself into the waves.

29

January 2015

"**S**HE LEFT A NOTE."

I looked at Kate Mueller, sitting across the table from me. From the pictures I had seen of Rhonda Harris, I'd say the daughter took more after her father.

I pushed the note in the small plastic bag across the table so she could see it. She leaned over and put on her glasses.

She read it, then looked up at me.

"What is that supposed to mean?" she asked. "Why would she write this? Why would she write I can't live with myself? I'm sorry? I don't quite understand. What did she do, Officer?"

I leaned forward in my chair. My wet hair fell onto my face. I removed the lock and pulled it all back. I thought for a second about my mother, who always wanted me to cut my hair, and now Abigail had started saying it too. But I liked having long hair, even if the girls in my life didn't think it was suitable for a detective.

My blood was still pumping fast through my veins from the surfing. The exhaustion was gone. I felt more alive than ever and more determined to solve this case than ever. Nothing like a good surf session to clear my brain.

"That's kind of what I was hoping you would clear up for me."

Kate Mueller shook her head. Her blond hair was set in a ponytail. Her face looked terrified.

"I don't believe any of this, Officer. My mother…my mother would never kill herself. She was so happy lately. The last couple of years, she has been so happy. We were going on a cruise next month. She invited us…she was the one who wanted to spend more time with her grandchildren."

"Can you verify it is her handwriting?"

"Yes. That is my mother's handwriting."

"Good. Now, returning to what you just said. I take it you wouldn't say she had been suicidal?"

"Not at all, Officer. Not at all. On the contrary." Kate Mueller's blue eyes stared intensely at me. "I have never seen her happier."

I wrote her statement on my notepad, then looked up at her again. "I hate to ask this, but I have to. Do you think she would be capable of committing murder?"

Kate Mueller looked at me, baffled. She put a hand to her chest. "Murder? You think that's what the note meant?"

"Her neighbor from across the street was found killed just two days ago. It does come off a little suspicious."

"I…I have never…no. Not my mother. She was the sweetest old lady. We might have had our differences, but not…that. She couldn't."

I nodded and wrote it down. I wasn't expecting her own daughter to tell me her mother was a murderer anyway, but I had to ask. I moved on with the interview.

"She used to work at Florida Today as a reporter, you say? But she retired early?"

"Yes. My mother was a writer. Always had been. Before she had me, she dreamt about being an author, but as you know, most people can't live off of that, so she had to work as a journalist for a living to support me. She was alone with me. My dad died when I was seven. Up until then, she hadn't worked a day in her life. But then she had to. She was lucky to get the job there, even though she didn't like it much."

"Why didn't she like it?"

Kate Mueller shrugged. "I don't know. She didn't like to have someone telling her what to write and what not to write. She wanted to make up her own stories."

"So, she liked to read as well, I assume. We found all of John Platt's books in her bedroom. Was she especially fond of him?"

Kate Mueller looked surprised. "Not that I know of," she said. "She never liked thrillers or mysteries much."

I showed her a picture of the many books spread on the rug and on her desk. "It seems to me she really enjoyed reading his books, don't you think?"

Kate Mueller stared at the photo, then back at me. "I don't know what to say to that. People change their taste, I guess."

"Okay," I said, and put the picture away. "You say she retired early. How come?"

"I...she was tired of working for the paper, so she told them she wanted to retire. I think it was good for her. She became a much happier person afterwards."

"And that was four years ago?"

"Yes."

"What did she do since?" I asked.

Kate Mueller shrugged again. "I don't know. I never visited her much. To be honest, we never had a real close relationship. I always sensed that she was bitter at me. You know, for making her quit her dream. It was because of me she had to stop writing books and trying to get them published. She had no choice when my dad died. I guess she kind of resented me for that."

"But, she did invite you on a cruise?" I asked.

"The last two years or so she has been trying to get back into my life. Last year, we all went to Paris together. She was the one who invited us and paid for everything, so I could hardly say no, even though my husband isn't that fond of my mother. And I guess I really wanted her to be a part of my children's lives. And, maybe...maybe I was hoping she would forgive me for ruining her life."

Kate Mueller sniffled. I saw tears pile in her eyes. I handed her a pack of tissues and poured her some water.

"How did she get the money for all this?" I asked. "A trip for five people to Paris isn't cheap. Neither is a cruise."

Kate Mueller shrugged again with a sniffle. "She said she had saved a lot of money up. Maybe her pension? I...I never thought to ask."

30

January 2015

"I think I'm going to leave John. I've already contacted a lawyer. I want out."

Melanie Schultz looked at her friends around the table at the restaurant. Sylvia gasped and almost choked on her Chardonnay.

"I thought you were happy with the way things were," she said, her voice trembling slightly.

Melanie shrugged and picked up a tomato with her fork and ate it. Her two-year-old son, Sebastian, was babbling something from his high chair. She gave him a piece of bread to nibble. It had been two hard years with him. She knew she was throwing a bomb on her friends.

"I'm not sure I can live like this anymore," she said. "I mean it's only a matter of time before he finds out about me and Pete, and then it's all over."

"But…but isn't there something we can do? Can't you solve it somehow?" Sylvia said, looking at the others for backup. "I really didn't think it would go this far. Maybe you're just being hasty here. I mean…you have to think it through, don't you? Have you thought about Sebastian?"

Melanie shrugged and ate another tomato from her salad. She really wasn't that fond of salads, and would have preferred to have a sandwich or a taco, but all the other girls always picked salads, and she didn't want to be the only one being unhealthy.

"He'll stay half the time with me and half with John, I guess."

"But, John is always traveling," Molly said. Her face was terrified, her lips tight. "I agree with Sylvia on this. I really think you should think it through."

"I have thought it through. Believe me. He'll just have to stay with me most of the time, then."

"Oh, it's going to crush John. You do realize that, right? It will completely crush him," Molly continued. "He loves Sebastian. And he absolutely adores you. He does everything for you. Do you really want to leave that?"

Melanie felt a pinch of guilt in her heart. Molly was right. That was why she hadn't left him before now. She knew it was going to kill him. He loved her to death. The problem was that she didn't love him back. Never had. She married him because it was the sensible thing to do, because he would take care of her, because that was the way her mother had raised her. All of her teenage years, she had told her how important it was to marry well, to make sure you found a husband that could support you so you didn't have to work. So you could stay home with the children and take care of the house.

But Melanie never really enjoyed staying home with Sebastian. She had liked it when she worked as a secretary at the big law firm in Orlando. She liked staying busy, having colleagues, and having something to do every day...places to be and people to talk to. She never enjoyed just taking care of her baby. She loved Sebastian, of course she did, but it wasn't what she wanted out of her life. She never wanted a loveless marriage and being a staying-at-home mom. She wanted more. She wanted to work. She wanted to go places. To see the world, to meet interesting people and eat exotic food. She wanted to be with grown-up people every day and talk about other things than her child and how to raise him or how to get rid of a rash or how to lose the baby weight while sipping Chardonnay.

There has to be more to adult life than this!

And now she had met a man she really liked. He made her life more interesting. She knew it was wrong, and felt so guilty about seeing him. But it wasn't just about the sex anymore. It was more. They had long talks afterwards. She liked talking to him. He was so interesting. Nothing like John. She was falling for Pete. She was starting to see him as her way out of her suburban boredom. She was going to talk to him about it today. Tonight, she was going to tell John. It was like ripping off a Band-Aid…the faster, the better.

"I know," she told her friends. "I know it's going to be hard, but it's what I want. I want to move on with my life. I hope John will understand. And I hope you will too."

She could tell by the look on her friends' faces that they didn't. They didn't want to. They all enjoyed their lives and didn't like the way she was suddenly questioning hers. It was written all over their faces.

We thought you were one of us.

31

January 2015

He was looking at her through the window of his truck. Melanie was her name. She was beautiful. Everything about her was so intoxicating. The Snakecharmer had been observing her for quite a while... months, actually. She and her friends always went to the same place for lunch on Wednesdays with their babies in their strollers. They ate Cobb salads and drank white wine while talking. The same procedure every Wednesday.

Her long painted fingernails were playing with her hair while she spoke to her friends in the parking lot outside the restaurant. They were saying their goodbyes. He rolled down his window and peeked out.

"Hey there," he said. "Can I give you girls a ride anywhere?"

They looked at one another and laughed. "In that thing?" one asked with a shiver.

The three of them shook their heads. The condescending look on their faces was saying, Who does he think he is? Why is he talking to us?

The Snakecharmer laughed. He pulled his arm inside the window.

"All right, ladies. Suit yourselves."

He backed out of the parking lot and drove off with a grin

on his face. He watched them shake their heads in his rearview mirror before he drove onto the street, took a right turn, then took a small street down and ended up in front of a big house in a nice neighborhood. He stopped the engine.

Then he waited.

Minutes later, he spotted the woman driving down the street in her brown Audi. She parked the car in the driveway and got out on her high heels. She grabbed the baby from the back seat and placed him on her hip. He smiled and watched her from afar. Such a gorgeous woman with such a perfect life. Such a shame.

"Yes, that's right. I know where you live, little bitch. I know everything about you."

He waited till she walked inside her house before he got out of the car, then he walked into the neighbor's yard, crawled over the wall, and landed in her yard. He knew his way around. He walked up to the back porch with the pool area and watched her through the large windows as she put the baby in a playpen. He hid while watching her open the sliding doors leading to the yard to let the cat out, leaving them open.

It was almost too easy.

He didn't have to wait long before the car drove up. He looked at his watch. It was two o'clock.

"Right on time, as usual, Your Honor," he mumbled, as he watched the judge get out of his black Cadillac Escalade and trot up the driveway wearing his black suit. He was looking over his shoulder to make sure no one saw him. Lucky for him, the driveway was surrounded by big walls, just as the entire house was. People always thought they were protecting themselves by putting up walls around their property, when in reality, they just made it easier for people like the Snakecharmer to act without risk of being seen.

He heard the doorbell ring, then the door open, and soon he saw the judge and the woman cuddled up in a warm embrace against the wall of the foyer.

He watched them through the big windows on the porch.

"I guess this court is now in session," he whispered. "The Honorable Judge Martin presiding."

As usual, he could see everything they did. As usual, he could follow their every move when the judge pulled up her skirt and threw her up against the wall. When she pulled down his pants and took him in her mouth. When he lifted her up and threw her on the dining room table and entered her from behind. Yes, everything up until now was just as usual on a Wednesday afternoon in Cocoa Beach.

But after this, nothing would be as usual for the two of them again.

The Snakecharmer picked up his gun, walked towards the sliding door, and walked inside. While he could hear the two of them moaning and groaning in the living room, on the couch, he crept up behind them, placed a gun to the judge's head and fired while yelling.

"All rise!!"

The woman beneath the judge screamed, terrified when the blood spurted into her face, then again when she spotted the familiar face above the lifeless body. The baby had woken up and was crying in his playpen.

"W...what...who...why...?" the woman stuttered, thinking somehow this must be a misunderstanding; somehow, he must have gotten it all wrong. She stared with disbelief at his face, waiting for some kind of explanation, but was struck with terror as she saw the dark chill in his eyes.

"Shhh..." he whispered, then stroked her beautiful face gently with his fingers. A small whimper emerged from her mouth. A tear escaped her eye. He caught it with his finger and looked at it. Then he picked up a pillow. He smiled at her with compassion and excitement, right before he forced it against her lips. She tried to fight him off with all her strength, but with no success. Her painted fingernails pierced through the skin on his arm.

32

January 2015

The Snakecharmer wrapped the body of Melanie into a blanket, then carried it out to his truck and put her in the back. Drago and Django hissed in their glass tank.

"Easy there, boys," he grinned. "This is Melanie. She will be riding with us today."

He grabbed a gas can, closed the back of the truck, and walked back to the house. He had driven the car into the driveway and closed the gate. No one would ever see him, and even if they did, they wouldn't wonder why he was there.

The Snakecharmer whistled as he walked back to the house with the can in his hand. Today was one of the good days. He had considered leaving something for the detectives to chew on. Something like lipstick painted on a mirror with a message or a note, but had decided that wasn't his thing. It was too risky. He wanted them to know he was the master. He was the one in charge, and if he started leaving little notes behind, then they would just end up tracking him down. And that wasn't part of his plan.

No, he had come up with something much better.

He walked inside and looked at the dead judge on the carpet. Bloodstains had completely ruined the light couch. He poured gasoline on the body of Judge Martin, then saluted him respectfully with a large grin before he grabbed his lighter and set him on fire. Still grinning, he walked to the playpen where the baby was crying. The Snakecharmer smiled at the young child, who was eager to be picked up and reaching his arms in the air. The Snakecharmer tilted his head while the heat from the flames behind him licked at his neck.

"Now, isn't that adorable?" he said.

The baby cried louder, still reaching up his arms. He smiled, then bent down and picked him up, right before he rushed out of the burning house.

He put the child in the passenger seat of the truck and strapped him down, then opened the gate and raced out of the driveway. Once he reached the end of the road, he heard a loud explosion behind him, and with a grin on his face, he watched the house go up in flames in the rearview mirror.

He imitated the sound of the explosion with his mouth, then looked at the child in the back.

"Mama?" the child said with a whimper.

The man shook his head. "No. Not mama. Dada. Can you say that? Dada? Mama is gone. She left us, Son. You know how it is. It's always the children that get hurt."

He stopped at a red light. A police car drove up on his side. The Snakecharmer pretended he didn't notice. Out of the corner of his eye, he watched the officer in the car. He was eating something while looking at the resorts to his right.

He didn't even look at the truck.

The man chuckled to himself, then looked at the baby. "They make it almost too easy."

While waiting for the light to turn, the man could tell the police officer got news over the radio. He looked perplexed, then put on the siren and tried to get out of the line of traffic. The Snakecharmer backed up to make room for the officer and let him drive through.

"Almost too easy," he repeated, as he watched the car disappear in the opposite direction down A1A and heard the many sirens approaching in the distance. "What do you say…Will?"

Yes, that's it. He looks like a Will.

The kid didn't react. He had stopped crying, though. Fire trucks and ambulances were blasting by in the opposite direction.

"Will it is, then."

33

January 1985

She had the baby. It took thirty-two hours of labor to get him out, but she had the baby. And Victor was right there all the time, holding her hand, wiping her forehead with a cold cloth, taking her aggressive comments, and loving her when she needed it.

He was there for her through everything.

When he came to take her and their son home, he told her he had a surprise for her.

"You're driving the wrong way," she said. "Our condo is in the opposite part of town."

"I told you I had a surprise," he said with a grin.

Annie really tried to like his smile, but his teeth were so crooked and yellow from too much coffee. His parents were loaded; why didn't he just get them fixed?

Lying in the hospital with her newborn, resting for days, regaining her strength, Annie had decided that if she was going to live with this man for the rest of her life, then she would have to try and make the best of what she had. At least he adored her. Maybe she could change him. People changed. She could get him to have his teeth done, she could get him to stop eating things that smelled bad, maybe use a better cologne. She could change the way he dressed. That was what women did, wasn't it? It had been done before, so of course she could.

They came closer to a gated neighborhood and Victor drove up to the booth. A uniformed man came out. When he saw Victor, he lifted his cap and opened the gate.

"Does he know you?" Annie asked.

Victor couldn't stop grinning. It didn't make him prettier. "He'll get to know you too. Soon."

Annie drew her brows together. What was this? Were they going to visit someone? Was he just showing her and the baby off? Because, if that was the case, then she certainly wasn't up for it.

"Victor…I don't think…"

Victor stopped her, then parked the car in front of a big house. Annie looked at it through the window. It was huge. No, it was humongous. And so beautiful. It looked just like a house she had once seen in a magazine.

"Who lives here?" she asked.

"Don't you recognize it?" he asked.

"It looks like…"

Victor pulled out the magazine and showed her. "One and the same," he said, smiling from ear to ear.

"You found the same house? How did you know? Why?" Annie asked, still not understanding what was going on.

"Yes. You showed it to me. Don't you remember? You said it was the most beautiful house you had ever seen."

"But…but that was months ago. How did you…remember?" Annie asked. Her voice was shivering.

"Nothing is too good for my baby," Victor said.

Annie's heart dropped. Could it be? What was he saying? "Do…do you mean…?"

No, it can't be!

Victor nodded, smiling from ear to ear. "Yes, darling. I bought it for you."

Annie found it hard to breathe. She couldn't believe what he was saying. Instead of saying anything, she shrieked and woke up the baby in the back seat.

"Oh, my God, Victor!"

She leaned over and kissed him, and for once, didn't care about his bad teeth or smell. "Oh, my God! Oh, my God! I love you, Victor!"

34

January 2015

I t looked like the end of the world. I could hardly believe my own eyes when I arrived at the scene on Country Club Road. It was late in the afternoon. Flames were still licking the sky. The heat was unbearable. Luckily, the wind carried the smoke out over the Banana River.

It had taken the firefighters hours to get the fire under control and make sure it wasn't threatening the neighboring houses. The fire still wasn't entirely put out, but at least it was contained. Neighbors had gathered in the street, watching the scene with terror in their eyes.

"That poor family," they whispered.

Usually, I was never called out to fires, but Weasel had asked me to come down. I was glad I had asked my mom to pick up the twins.

"So, they got it under control, I hear?" I said.

Weasel nodded. She was wearing her hair in a ponytail today. It looked great. "Took a while, but yes. The entire house burned down, though. They can put it out, they say, but not save it."

I took in a deep breath. The family had lost everything, then. "So, why did you want to talk to me?"

Weasel looked at her shoes, then up at me. "I spoke to the husband. He was on a business trip in Southern Florida. He got here an hour ago. He says his wife and child are missing. He's been calling her. He talked to all of her friends, who she met with for lunch, and they said she went home. With the baby."

My heart stopped. "You think…you think they were in the house?"

Weasel shrugged. "I don't know what I think anymore. But I thought you should know."

I nodded. It was what they would call a suspicious death. That was my field. "Got it. Anything else I should know?"

Weasel looked at me. "No. Go on home to those beautiful kids of yours. Kiss them for me, will you?"

I chuckled. Weasel never had kids of her own. I often wondered if she regretted her decision.

"Sure thing." While I spoke, the firefighters finally managed to put out the last few flames. The spectators clapped, and so did I. They were the true heroes around here. First responders in most situations. They never knew what would await them when they arrived.

"Chief!" I heard the Captain of the fire department yell, addressed to Weasel. He approached her, holding something between his hands. "We found this."

"A gas can," I said. "Where did you find it?"

"In the driveway. Next to that burnt out car over there."

"Was that the wife's car?" I asked. "There seem to be two."

Weasel looked pensive. "The husband said she drove a brown Audi."

"That's not a brown car," I said. "Anyone can see that, even from where we're standing. It might have been burned, but that car was black."

I walked closer and spotted the license plate. It was still sitting in its place. I kneeled next to it, careful not to step on anything. Weasel was behind me.

"Could you run this plate for me, please?" I asked.

"Sure thing." Weasel grabbed her radio and ran the plate. Then she looked at me while shaking her head. "It belongs to

Judge Pete Martin." Weasel went pale. "What the...what is Judge Martin's car doing here?"

"Maybe he was visiting?"

"You think he was in there as well? Oh, my God." Weasel clasped her face. I couldn't blame her for being upset. "What the heck is going on around here?" she asked, looking at me like I had an answer for everything.

"I don't know," I said. "But I can tell you one thing. Someone set this house on fire. And that someone wanted us to know it was on purpose."

35

January 2015

Weasel and I drove in my Jeep together to get to Judge Martin's house. He lived in one of the newer houses in Cocoa Isles, overlooking the Thousand Islands. His wife opened the door.

"Mrs. Martin?" I asked and showed her my badge.

"Yes?" She looked from me to Weasel and back. The terror was in her eyes. It seemed like she already suspected something was wrong. "Weslie? What's going on here?"

"We're looking for Pete," Weasel said.

"He's not here. He was supposed to be home hours ago. I called his cell, but..." she stopped herself. Her eyes were flickering back and forth between us. "Did something happen?"

"We don't know yet, ma'am," I said. "But we did locate his car."

"His car? Where?"

I took in a deep breath. Weslie was personal friends with the judge and his wife. It was best if I told her. I didn't have emotions involved. "It was parked in the driveway of a house that burned down this afternoon. We still don't..."

I didn't get any further before she broke down and cried. "Oh, no!" She clasped her mouth. "I mean, I heard the sirens…I watched it on TV. The news chopper showed every-thing. I wondered…I knew…"

"Could you tell us what your husband might be doing there?" I asked.

"He…he…he was visiting…he thought I didn't know, but I did. It has been going on for months. I let him. Thought he would figure out that he wasn't really missing out on anything, that he had all he needed at home, if you understand what I mean…It wasn't like it was his first. He always comes back… he always…oh, my…if you'll excuse me, I need to…sit down."

I grabbed her arm before she fell and helped her inside the hallway. I found a chair and helped her sit down.

"Just take it easy, Mrs. Martin," I said. "We don't know that anything has happened to him yet."

Weasel held her hand while Mrs. Martin sobbed, then bit her lip to hold it back. "It's all my fault. I should have stood up to him. I should have told him I knew. Told him to end it as soon as I found out. I even drove over there to see her. She was gorgeous. And so much younger than me. How was I supposed to compete? All I could do was to give him a stable home to come back to and hope he would know not to throw that away, you know?"

I exhaled. "I know," I said. "You did the best you could."

Mrs. Martin choked on a cry. It was hard for her to breathe properly. "You shouldn't be alone," Weasel said. "Do you want me to call your sister to come?"

Mrs. Martin nodded with a sob. "That would be very nice, thank you. I need to call the kids as well. They're upstate. They deserve to know."

"Maybe you should wait with that till we know what happened," Weasel suggested. "The technicians are working the scene right now, and hopefully we'll know more soon."

Mrs. Martin looked up at Weasel. "Technicians? As in crime scene technicians? You think it was arson?"

Weasel nodded. "We're pretty certain. We found a can of gasoline on the scene."

Mrs. Martin gasped and held a hand to her chest. Then, she finally broke down and let the tears roll across her face. Weasel called for the sister while I found a box of tissues in the bathroom and handed it to her. She thanked me and wiped her eyes. "I'm so sorry. I feel horrible that you have to see me like this. It's all just so…"

"Unbelievable. I know," I said.

36

January 2015

Two days later, Weasel called me into her office. It was right before lunch and I was planning on hitting the Juice 'N Java within a few minutes when she spoiled my plans.

"Shut the door," she said with a serious face.

"I take it you have news?" I asked and sat down.

She sighed and hid her face between her hands for a second before she looked at me again. "It was him. They finally identified the body found in the burned down house. It was Judge Martin."

"Jeez. Well, at least the family will finally get closure," I said. "Did you tell his wife yet?"

"I'm going over there after this meeting. Just trying to gather myself a little first."

"I understand. What about the mother and child?"

She threw a file on the desk in front of me. "According to this, they found remains of just one body. They used dental records to ID him."

"At least that gives us hope for the mother, Melanie Schultz, and her child," I said and flipped through the pages in the file. Pictures of the carbonized body parts jumped out at me. They had found bullets on the scene too. And then the can of gasoline. They believed it had been poured on the body of the judge. The fire started in the living room.

"Yeah, well. With fires, you never know. But, yes. I have a feeling the mother and child weren't in the house," she said. "I just can't for the life of me...understand what the judge was doing in the house all by himself?"

"It sounds odd. Maybe he was waiting for her to come home. What we know now is they usually met at two o'clock every Wednesday. Her friends have told us and so has Mrs. Martin, who knew all about it. Maybe Melanie Schultz just never made it home?"

Weasel slammed her palm on the table. "But the car, Jack. Her car was right there." She pointed at the file in my hand. "It was in the driveway. She drove home, but then what? She decided to go for a walk? She was picked up by someone? She took a cab out of town and disappeared? What?"

"I don't know. Let's stick to what we do know. The judge. Who do we think would want to kill the judge?" I asked.

Weasel snorted. "Look around. A lot of people. There's an election coming up. His poster is in most people's front yard. He had many supporters around here, but also many opponents. He put criminals in jail. It could be political. It could be revenge. You pick. There's a lot to choose from. There are many people with motives."

"Like his wife," I said.

"Don't get cocky."

"I'm not. I'm serious," I said. "The man was cheating on her repeatedly. That gives her a pretty good motive in my book."

"I've known the woman since we were children. It's not her," Weasel growled.

"We have to at least look into it," I said. "And you know it."

"Good grief. Okay then, but be careful with her, all right? She's in a fragile state of mind."

"I'm always gentle," I said and smiled. "So, are we looking at a connection on the three deaths here?" I asked.

Weasel shook her head. "I talked to Sheriff Ron earlier, and we both agree there is no need to look into that angle. Nothing connects them, apart from the fact that they were committed in our town within a close time frame. I think it's just a coincidence. There is nothing that indicates they're related. One of the deaths is a suicide, so that is certainly not connected to the others."

I wasn't sure I agreed, but didn't say it out loud.

"What about the man Melanie's friends said they saw at the parking lot at the restaurant right after they were done eating?" I asked. "I can't seem to get him out of my mind."

"The Animal Control guy?" Weasel asked.

"Yes. They said he was driving one of the vans from Animal Control and had snakes in a tank inside the van. He offered them a ride, they told us. One of the girls took a look inside and saw the snakes."

Weasel nodded. "Joel called Animal Control, and they told him they didn't have a guy in that area on that date." She looked at me pensively. "You think he might have followed her back to the house?"

I shrugged. "I have no idea at this point. But I think we should have a drawing made and send it to the newspaper and ask the public to help us find this guy. Tell them we'd like to talk to him."

Weasel nodded. "I'll set that in motion. The friends said they got a pretty good look at him. They can help us get a good picture of this Snake-guy. What else? How are we on the suicide and the homicide on West Bay Drive?"

"Nothing much to tell yet," I said. "I'm looking into Rhonda Harris' finances. She made quite a lot of money the last couple of years. I'm trying to figure out where the money came from."

"Good. But don't spend too much time on the West Bay Drive case. The murder of the judge has first priority now, and finding Melanie Schultz and her child. Judge Martin was a high-profile judge around here. People will be demanding justice. I know the Mayor will. It's going to create quite the media-drama once they get the news. I'm not looking forward to that part."

I got up from my chair, holding the file in my hand. "I want to take a closer look at it anyway," I said.

"By all means. It's your case now. Knock yourself out."

"Thanks," I said, and walked towards the door. I grabbed the handle and looked back at Weasel. "And don't worry. I think you look great on TV."

I ducked just in time to avoid the stapler hitting me.

37

April 1990

She had everything she could ever ask for in life. She had the most beautiful house in a gated area, she had the biggest most expensive car, and the most beautiful jewelry that Victor brought home for her almost every month just to spoil her.

She had everything, her neighbors said, with jealousy in their voices. Even her child was beautiful. Her little baby boy, who was now five years of age, was just so…so perfect.

Why wasn't she happy? Why wasn't Annie enjoying any of it? Why did she constantly feel like she was trapped in a prison and couldn't breathe?

Why?

She asked herself that very question every day when Victor kissed her goodbye with those yellow crooked teeth and bad breath of his, and she was left alone with the child. She never knew what to do with him. To be honest, she found it hard to spend time with him, and often she would leave him downstairs with some toys, then walk upstairs and go back to sleep or just hide. She didn't know what it was about the child, but she just didn't like to be close to him. She feared it was because of how he had come to be. Did she resent him for it? Did she somehow blame him for the rape?

She didn't know. All she knew was that she was counting

the days till he would start Kindergarten after the summer. Then, Annie wouldn't have to be with him all day. Finally, she would be able to have some time for herself.

While sitting in her bathrobe in her bedroom, listening to the boy play with his toys downstairs, smashing cars into each other and pretending they exploded, she wondered if she even loved him.

Victor adored the kid. There was no doubt about it. He loved the boy. But Annie found it harder and harder. When she looked at his face, she sometimes thought she saw Tim's eyes, or one of his friend's facial expressions. And that was when she was reminded of what had happened on that dreadful night six years ago.

Two years ago, she had confided everything to her mother. She hadn't been able to hold it in anymore, and just told her everything. She asked her if she was a terrible mother because she found it hard to look at her own child.

Hoping her mother would understand her, she had leaned against her shoulder, longing for a comforting hug, but her mother had, instead, moved away and turned her back on her. She had walked to the kitchen sink and started peeling potatoes while saying:

"Well at least everything turned out fine, right? At least you have a good husband now, and you live a great life in that big house. I tell you, I've never had a house like that. You should be very grateful and not dig up all these ugly memories. Make the best of what you've got. That's what I always say. That's how you get by; that's how you live a good life."

Annie had stared at her mother's back while she spoke. While tears streamed across her cheeks and the feeling of abandonment pierced her stomach, she imagined grabbing that potato peeler out of her mother's hand and piercing her in the heart with it. She wondered what it would feel like and closed her eyes to shut out her mother's words. They felt like punches to her stomach.

Since then, Annie had stopped seeking her parents' comfort and understanding. While her discomfort in that big mansion grew day by day, she wondered if anyone would even care if she died.

"Victor would," she mumbled to herself and shivered in disgust. The more the days passed with him, the more she couldn't stand being close to him. She always dreaded having sex with him and tried to get out of it if he suggested or tried to make a move when they went to bed. There was always a headache or a tiredness to blame it on. Every now and then, she gave in to him, simply because she felt she had to, since he had done so much for her, and let his stinking sweaty body on top of hers. She would close her eyes and think of something else while he finished his business. Lately, she had started to gain a lot of weight, trying to make herself less attractive to him, and it seemed to be working. So, she continued. Sitting in her bedroom during the day, she stuffed herself with chocolate, cheesecake, chips, and sodas. Soon Victor stopped making approaches on her at night at all. It was a small victory for her, but it didn't help with the child. She still wasn't happy, and she blamed the boy.

"Soon," she whispered, sitting in her bedroom, while he played wildly downstairs, knocking over furniture and jumping on the couch. "Soon, he'll be gone all day, and then you'll be able to enjoy your life. Then you'll be happy."

38

January 2015

W e had a drawing made of the snake-guy and it was published in all the local papers and shown on TV, along with pictures of Melanie and Sebastian Schultz. According to Melanie's friends, the guy was both long-haired and long-bearded. He wore his hair in a ponytail. It got a lot of immediate response from the public, but unfortunately, nothing we could use.

As Monday morning came and went, I feared more and more for the life of Melanie and her child. I had hoped they had just gone somewhere else, maybe visited family or friends we didn't know about, and then maybe would see this on TV and call us. But nothing came of it.

On Tuesday, I finally had a breakthrough in the suicide of Rhonda Harris. The bank tracked her big payments over the last couple of years and found them to be coming from across the street, from Laura Bennett's bank account. And they were quite large amounts. Hundreds of thousands of dollars several times a year.

"Why was Laura Bennett paying Rhonda Harris?" I asked Weasel, when we went for lunch at Juice N' Java across the street.

"Ask the husband," she said.

So, I did. I called him and asked him to come down to the

station. He arrived in the afternoon. I hadn't seen him since I had been at the hospital to interview him. He looked a lot better now. He was dressed nicely in a white shirt and black pants. He had trimmed his moustache and cut his hair nicely, making him look a little like a young Tom Selleck. He didn't look like the drunk everybody was so busy making him into. But some drunks hid it well. I smelled no alcohol on his breath, though.

"Haven't touched a drink since it happened," he said, as if he could read my mind. He sat down. "Haven't gambled either."

"Good to hear. So, how's Ben?" I asked. I knew he was back in school, since Abigail and Austin had told me. They had all tried to be a good friend to him, they said. I liked that.

"He's better," Brandon Bennett said. "It hasn't been easy, but people have been good to us. They're taking real good care of him at the school."

"That's good to know," I said. "That's what I've always liked about this town. We take care of each other here in Cocoa Beach."

"So, how can I help you, Detective?" Brandon asked. "Is there any news about my wife's murder?"

He hit me right in my guilty spot. I had been dealing mostly with the murder of the judge lately, and I had to put the Bennett killing a little to the side. I wasn't proud of it.

"Not much, no, but I do have something I need to ask you about," I said. I placed the bank statement in front of him. I had underlined the big transfers of money to Rhonda Harris's account.

"What am I looking at?" Brandon Bennett said.

"It has come to my attention that your wife paid your neighbor across the street a lot of money several times a year. Do you know why?"

Brandon Bennett shook his head. "This is news to me as well," he said. "Why would she do that?"

"That's what I'm asking you."

He exhaled. "As much as I would love to help, I have no

idea. This is a huge surprise to me as well. I'm sorry, Detective. Have you asked Rhonda Harris's daughter? She might know."

"I have. She didn't know either. And you're sure you didn't know about this?" I asked.

"Positive."

"What about her brother?"

"What about him?"

"You said they stayed in contact. How much contact was that?" I asked.

Brandon Bennett shrugged. "I don't know, Detective. Not much. I knew he called every now and then. She visited him a few times. I remember he came on the night of the murder. I remember he was angry and they went outside to discuss something. She didn't want him there. She asked him to leave, but he wouldn't. He told her he needed money. She said he had enough. Then they went outside and I didn't hear any more. I guess she made him leave, because she returned alone. I asked her what it was about, but she told me it was none of my business. That's when we started fighting. She told me I couldn't go out on the casino boats anymore. I had spent too much money lately. I felt like a child when she spoke to me like that. So, I got angry and told her it was all her fault I was drinking and gambling."

"Because of the child."

Brandon Bennett looked at the floor. "Yes. I couldn't stand being at the house. I couldn't stand being close to her when I felt that way. When I felt like she hadn't been able to care enough for our child."

"Sudden Infant Death Syndrome isn't anyone's fault," I said. "No more than an accident usually is, or a heart-attack."

Brandon Bennett shook his head. "I know…I know…It's just…" He looked up.

"It's just what?" I asked. "You needed someone to blame? We all do when bad things happen. It makes it easier to handle. But, it often destroys our relationships." I sighed and let it go. How Brandon Bennett chose to deal with his loss was his choice. "So, do you believe Laura might have hidden something from you? Was something going on between her and her brother?"

"He asked for money a lot. I think that was all. I think Laura felt guilty because she had gotten the entire inheritance. He couldn't take care of himself properly, and she believed she needed to help him out. But he never stopped. I guess that's why she got angry with him."

"You think he could have killed her?" I asked.

"Peter? I don't know. I'm not an expert on killers, Detective."

I chatted with Brandon Bennett for a little while longer, but didn't get anything more out of him. I asked him if he remembered any more from the night of the murder, and he told me that he was slowly regaining some memory, but still nothing that would help the investigation. Nothing between midnight Sunday night and waking up at the hospital Tuesday morning. I kept wondering who could have slipped him that drug in his drink and asked him if he had any friends or anyone he suspected could do such a thing.

"I...I really don't, Detective."

I wasn't getting anywhere, so I sent him away, then put the papers aside and grabbed myself another cup of coffee. I wondered about the brother, Peter. He was beginning to look more and more like a suspect in my eyes. I watched the cars go by outside my window, while also wondering what had been going on between the neighbors. Rhonda Harris's suicide note had said I can't live with myself. What did that refer to? Did she kill Laura? Was she blackmailing her or something? Was she demanding money from her, and when she refused to give her more, she killed her? If so, then what was she blackmailing her about?

There was a knock on my door and Joel Hall peeked in. "Detective? I'm sorry to interrupt, but I have something I need to tell you."

"Come on in. Grab a chair."

"It was just something I thought about last night," Joel

said and sat. "Last year, there was a woman in here. She was complaining about John Platt's latest book."

I leaned forward in my chair, then sipped some more coffee. "Complaining? About what?"

"I was the one who took her report. She wanted to file a report against the estate after John Platt died," she said.

I frowned. "Why? Had they committed a crime?"

"She claimed the books weren't written by John Platt. She said they weren't right or something. I never really listened. I pretended to file the report, but never did. It didn't make much sense, what she said. To be honest, I thought she was a wacko. But I thought you should know anyway."

January 2015

_____

"Someone called for Animal Control? I understand you had a snake in your garage?"

The Snakecharmer smiled from ear to ear. The woman opening the door was in her early thirties.

"Yes," the woman said with a deep sigh. "Thank you so much for coming this fast. I just got off the phone a few minutes ago. I was going crazy just thinking about it being out there."

She shivered.

The Snakecharmer looked at the goose bumps on her neck. A thrill went through his body. He thought about killing her right there on the spot, in the hallway of her own house. Just for the thrill of it.

"Let me show you the way," she said. "I think we better go through from the inside. I don't want it to run out into the yard and hide there if I open the garage door. I want it off the property, if you know what I mean."

"Of course, ma'am. I understand. And I take it you have children? I saw the bike in the driveway."

"Yes, she said. "We have a girl."

"We don't want her to get scared by one of those bastards while playing in the yard, now do we?"

The woman shivered again. She was so elegant when she

moved, so feminine. The Snakecharmer loved that. Like a gazelle in the savannah. And she was his prey. Just like the predator in the wild, he was watching her every move without her noticing it.

"Nice house you have here," he said, and followed her through the kitchen.

"Yes, thank you."

"What does your husband do?"

"He's a lawyer. Well, actually, we're getting a divorce, so…"

The Snakecharmer froze. He forced a smile. "I see. Well, that's too bad. I mean, it seems like you have everything here. It's always so hard on the children."

The woman sighed. The Snakecharmer felt the blood rush rapidly through his veins. He wanted so badly to snap her beautiful long neck. Talking about the divorce made the furor rise in him. Almost to the point where he was afraid he might snap.

Not now, you fool. Not now.

"I know," she said, and opened the door leading to the garage. "It's in here. I saw it over there by the cupboards. It had a lot of colors. That's how I knew it was one of the bad ones. You know how the saying goes."

"Red touch yellow, kills a fellow. Red touch black, friend of Jack," the Snakecharmer said. "People never remember it right."

"I know," she said with a light laugh. "I can never get it right either. But I definitely saw yellow on it."

"I'll take care of it, ma'am, don't worry."

"I'm glad," she said.

"Oh, and I do hope that there isn't another person involved."

"What was that?"

"An affair. I hope there isn't a third party involved," he said with a smirk. "It always gets nastier if there is."

The woman looked baffled. "I…I don't think that is any of your business. Now, if you'll just catch the snake."

"Of course, ma'am," he said.

"Say, haven't I seen you before?" she asked.

"Only if you've had other problems with snakes, ma'am," the Snakecharmer said, then turned his head away.

"I must be confusing you with someone else, then," she said and closed the door.

The Snakecharmer cursed while walking to the cupboards, grabbing the Coral snake by the tail and pulling it out. "Get out of there, Drago. Playtime is over."

He grabbed it by its mouth and petted it gently while talking to it. "Yes, you did a good job in here. Yes, of course, this woman needs to get what she deserves. What all of them deserve for doing what they do. For ruining EVERYTHING! I know she recognized me. Must be more careful now mustn't we? Those ugly pictures on TV are ruining everything, aren't they? Well, maybe a better disguise would help. Maybe another wig? One that isn't longhaired. Lose the fake beard, huh? Maybe another color of contacts. What's that, Drago? Yes, you're right. We need a new mummy now, don't we?" He laughed at his own little word play. Mummy/mommy. It was funny. "Yes, we do. But not now. Not yet. We must be patient, Drago. We must be patient."

40

January 2015

Tracey Burden was a big woman, who in many ways reminded me of Kathy Bates in Misery. The comparison didn't stop there, unfortunately. As I followed her into the living room of her house in Titusville, I realized she was just as crazy as well. She was wearing a fluttering colorful dress covered with butterflies. Her hair was put up with butterfly clips and the walls of her living room were decorated with pinned up butterflies, roaches, and spiders.

"I just love bugs," she exclaimed, as I walked inside. "Don't you?"

"Don't we all?" I said, and sat on her plastic-covered couch. I lied. If there was one thing I hated, it was bugs. Butterflies were okay, but the rest I could live without.

"I'm sorry about the plastic, but my cats keep scratching the fabric," she said and smiled. "Can I get you some coffee?"

"I'm good. Thank you."

The big woman sat down across from me. "I'm just so glad someone is finally taking my complaints seriously," she said, almost whispering like it was a secret. "I mean, it's been going on for years. And no one seems to want to listen."

"What has been going on?" I asked.

She looked puzzled. "Well, the forgery, of course. What else did you think I was talking about?"

She looked at me with those slightly wacky eyes. I exhaled and tried to focus. Her house was located on the mainland and had a small yard with dozens of garden gnomes that reminded me of that movie I'd seen with the kids, that Gnomeo and Juliet. Strange movie, I thought. Almost as strange as the woman sitting in front of me.

"BOO!"

I jumped in my seat. Tracey Burden laughed loudly and slapped her leg. "You were away in dreamland there, Detective," she said with a shrill voice. "Can't go around daydreaming on the job, can we?"

"I'm sorry. I've been working some long days," I said, beginning to regret having come here. When investigating murder, you often came upon some really strange types. It always brought out the weirdos.

"I bet. You have a lot to do, don't you? Lots of wackos out there. You sure you don't want any of that coffee?"

"No, I'm good. But I would like to know more about this presumed forgery you're talking about."

"Presumed? Now, I have never. Let me tell you something, Detective. There is nothing presumed about it. I can prove that John Platt hasn't written a word in the last three books that were published in his name. I'm his biggest fan. You might even say I'm his number one fan."

She laughed.

"Really? And how can you prove that he didn't write them?" I asked.

Tracey Burden got up. She picked two books from a shelf. Then she opened them and sat down. She placed the books in front of us. "This is one of the new books; this is one of the old ones. Look at them," she said.

I was wasting my time, but tried to look at the pages anyway.

"It jumps right out at ya', doesn't it?" she asked with a scoff. "They must think we're stupid. It was so obvious; I knew right away. I even created a Facebook-group for others like me who have detected it."

"I…I'm not sure I can see what it is," I said. "Could you help me out here? I'm not that big a John Platt fan."

Tracey Burden scoffed again and shook her head. "Look here and here," she said and pointed. "Look at that description right there. John Platt could never have written that. He actually describes this woman nicely. She is a nice person."

"And?"

"Everyone knows John Platt hates women, and that he always describes them as awful people. Especially since, the older he got, the meaner he was towards women. Someone must have hurt him badly in his life. But, suddenly, after his death, three more books came along where the women suddenly are heroes. That's not something John Platt would write. He was known to hate women. No, hate is too nice a word for it. He loathed them. That was all part of the fun. That's what made his books special."

"So, you're saying he didn't write these books? Then, who did?"

Tracey Burden lit up in a big smile. "Well, I guess that's your job to find out, isn't it, Detective?"

41

January 2015

I had no idea what to do with the information that Tracey Burden had given me. At first, I was simply glad to get out of there. She was a nutcase, and my first instinct was to just forget what she had said and move on. She had hardly provided proof of anything. Yet, it had still aroused my interest. I made some phone calls and tried to look into the matter, but was only met by a wall of silence from the publishing house and lawyers. That wasn't the way to approach this. I let it go for a while and went home to my family. My friends, Eliza and Tom, had invited us over for dinner. They had a child in the twins' class. I had told Emily she could stay home if she wanted.

"So, how are things?" Eliza asked, when she put the bowl of mashed potatoes on the table. "How are you holding up?"

Tom brought me a beer, while the twins scooped mashed potatoes onto their plates and started making volcanoes with the gravy, using their fingers as cars driving down the sides. I was too tired to ask them to stop playing with their food.

"I'm fine. Busy week, but I'm good."

"That's good, Jack. Being busy is good," Eliza said with a compassionate smile. She worried about the kids and me. I always spent most of our dinners together assuring her we were all surviving. It could be exhausting, since she didn't seem to believe me. Or maybe she just saw right through me. The fact was, I still loved Arianna. I still thought about her every hour of the day and wondered if I would ever hear from her again. I still jumped when the phone rang and a small voice inside of me said it could be her. It could be.

Even after four years.

Eliza and Tom had been my friends since we moved here. Well, actually they were our friends, since they went all the way back to when Arianna was still part of my life. Our kids went to preschool together. Eliza was friends with Arianna before she decided to leave. We used to live in the same condominium, and they were pregnant at the same time. She was in shock when Arianna left me. Maybe even more than I was, I sometimes thought.

"Still no word from her?" she asked me every time we saw each other, even now, four years later. We were done eating and moved to the living room, where Tom and I finished our beers. Tom's longboard was leaned up against the wall. I knew it had been a while since he last used it. Between his job at the bank and the family, it was hard for him to find time to hit the waves. Plus, Eliza didn't like it. She thought he spent too much time on the water. Time he could spend on doing things around the house they had just bought.

I shook my head. "No. And, frankly, I don't care anymore, Eliza," I lied.

"But, it's just so odd. So unlike her to just leave and not even check in on you every now and then. I mean, she cared about the twins. I just know she did. What kind of woman leaves her children when they're less than two years old?"

"She was depressed," I said and sipped my beer. I hated always having to defend Arianna.

"She didn't know what she was doing."

"I think she knew very well…" Eliza mumbled.

"What was that?" I asked.

Eliza annoyed me a little. She was always on Arianna's case. I was angry with Arianna for leaving us, of course I was, but I had stopped blaming her a long time ago. I had decided she simply wasn't well.

Eliza received a look from Tom. She shook her head with a sigh. "I know, I know," she said, and leaned back on the leather couch. "We can't say anything."

She paused and looked angrily at Tom. "I just think he deserves to know."

Tom gesticulated. "Why? Eliza? Why now?"

"Because he deserves to know the truth. It has been long enough, don't you think?"

I was starting to get alarmed over their little quarrel. Something was going on here. Exactly what was it I didn't know?

"Could you please just tell me what's going on here?" I asked.

Tom sighed and ran a hand through his hair. "Now see what you've done. Now we have to tell him."

"Tell me what?" I was holding the beer bottle tightly between my hands. "Tell me what, God dammit!"

Eliza looked at me. She took in a deep breath. "She was cheating on you," she said. "There, I said it. Arianna was seeing another guy behind your back. It went on for months. That's why she left. She needed time to think. She told me about it on the day before she left you. I always thought she'd come back. She told me she believed she would come back as soon as she had the time to figure things out. If not for you, then for the kids. She loved those kids, Jack, she really did. She was just so confused."

I put my beer down, then got to my feet. Abigail and Austin were playing in Amy's room. I called them and grabbed my leather jacket without another word. The kids came running out into the hallway.

Tom and Eliza came out to us. "Jack...I..." Tom said, then stopped.

"Not now, Tom," I said. "I'm not quite in the mood for this right now."

I felt so many things I couldn't put words to them. Anger,

betrayal, abandonment. How could they have kept this a secret for this long? My best friends?

"We were trying to protect you," Tom said, like he was reading my mind. "We thought you'd been through enough…"

I shook my head in disbelief. I was about to leave when it struck me. I turned and looked at Eliza. "I do have one question."

"Yes?"

"Who was he? Who was the bastard seeing my wife?"

42

March 1995

"I need to see my son."

Victor's mother barely looked at Annie as she stormed past her in the foyer of their house. Annie stared after her.

"He's in the study, working," Annie yelled, then decided she didn't care if she found him or not. She returned to the living room, where she put her feet back up and turned on the TV. She grabbed the container of ice cream and returned to her binging. Her sweats had gotten tight around the waist again. Soon, she would have to move up yet another size.

The boy was in his room doing whatever he wanted to do, and this was Saturday, her day of watching reruns of ER. No one, not even Victor's dramatic mother should ruin that. Watching that George Clooney as Dr. Ross nonstop was her treat; it was her drug from the reality of her life being so boring she could hardly bear it.

The voices coming from the study were getting louder. Annie could hear Victor's mom yelling, and suddenly, her interest was aroused. Victor's mother never yelled. She hardly ever showed any emotions except for contempt.

Something was going on.

Annie turned down the volume. She didn't have to hear to

watch George Clooney. She had seen every episode anyway; the storyline wasn't important.

"I'm telling you, Victor. You will do this, or I swear…" She heard Victor's mother say.

"You swear to do what, exactly, Mother?" Victor yelled back.

Uh-oh. This was bad. Victor never yelled either. What on earth was going on?

"I swear…I'll…we'll…and your father and I agree on this," she said.

Annie could only imagine how she was spitting and hissing. It sounded like it. This was better than any soap.

"What do you agree on?" Victor yelled.

"We'll take everything, Victor. The company. The house. Everything. You know we can. It's all in our names."

Annie almost dropped the ice cream bucket. Her heart started racing in her chest. What the heck was this? Annie got up from the couch and walked towards the study. The boy was so quiet in his room. She never knew what he did in there. To be honest, she didn't care. She cared less and less about the boy and never spent any time with him, if she could avoid it. He seemed to be fine without her.

"You won't do that," Victor said. "You can't do that to us. To me? I have a family here? We love the house?"

"Oh, you better believe we can and will do that, Victor. You lied to us all these years. Your entire marriage is based on a lie. Believe me when I say that if you don't divorce that… that tramp out there, then we're done with you. You are no longer our son."

Annie stopped breathing. A lump in her throat started to grow, and she felt like crying. Victor's mother was right, wasn't she? Annie was nothing but a tramp. Their marriage was a lie.

"Well, I don't care what you say, Mother. I love her. I love Annie. I love our son, and I love our life together. If you can't handle that, then…well then, take your money, your house, your company, and leave!"

Victor's mother gasped. "Victor!"

"That's right, Mother. I chose my family. I chose my wife. Even if that means we have to be poor. That's how much I love them."

Annie had to find a chair to sit down. She waddled backwards and stumbled into one and sat just as Victor's mother yelled.

"Fine. Have it your way." The door opened and she stormed out of the study. She took one glance at Annie, then stuck up her nose and disappeared.

Victor came out a second later. "Sweetie," he said to Annie. "You're all pale. Are you all right?"

"I...I..." she stuttered.

"You heard it? Well, don't worry. She found out about the boy not being mine. She wanted me to divorce you, but I would never do that."

Annie looked into Victor's eyes. It was hard to breathe. "But...but does that mean we have to be poor now, Victor?"

Victor laughed. "Yes. For a little while. They own the company; you know that. I was supposed to take over eventually, but we don't need that. I'll get another job. I'll start my own company."

"But...but the house? I love our house."

"I do too. But we'll get another one. I'll work hard to keep my baby happy. Don't worry, my love. We have each other and that's all I need."

Then he leaned over and kissed her, flashing his crooked teeth. She was repulsed by his breath.

"Our love is all we need," he said.

She wasn't so sure it was enough.

43

January 2015

Steven Williams! Steven freaking Williams! Of all people. Her boss. Arianna's boss. She had worked at an advertising agency after the twins had started preschool. She had enjoyed getting out of the condo and talking to grown up people, she had told me. I thought it had been good for her. I thought it had been a good idea, a way to get over her growing depression and sense of meaninglessness in her life. She needed to work; she had always worked, even before I met her, and needed it, I told myself. Needed a sense of purpose, a reason to get out of bed in the morning, a way to stay busy.

And then it turned out she had just been screwing around behind my back? I couldn't believe it. Here I had been busy making excuses for her, telling people she couldn't help herself, defending her, telling them she was sick and needed to get away to overcome this depression.

I couldn't sleep at all that night, and the following day I called the station and told them I would be late. I had no idea where I was going, but suddenly, I found myself parking the Jeep outside the agency's office. I sat in the car for maybe an hour, just staring at the building, feeling the anger rise in me, but still restraining myself from going in. I had no idea how I would react if I did.

Suddenly, I spotted Steven Williams in the parking lot. He had just walked out of the building, flanked by two other suit-wearing men with perfect hair. I watched them while they spoke, all carrying briefcases.

"What the heck did you see in this guy, Arianna?" I asked myself. Was it just the fact that he was everything I'm not? Was it because he had a stable life, a desk-job with no danger, good income, wore a tie to work, didn't have a crumple in his pants, not a spot on his shirt? Was that why? Or was it the excitement? Did she love him? Or was it just sex?

"Goddammit, Arianna. Why would you do this to your family? Didn't you know how much we loved you?"

I felt tears of anger press behind my eyes, thinking about all the wonderful weekends we spent together on the beach playing in the sand, throwing the Frisbee, flying kites, and picnicking in the sand. All the while, she was seeing this guy behind my back. I knew it was self-torture, but I couldn't stop wondering. Where had they done it? At his house? No, he probably wasn't stupid enough to risk that. Had they taken a room at a motel?

While thinking about it, the demon of anger got the better of me. I simply couldn't just stay in my car. I got out and stormed across the street without even looking for cars. Steven Williams was laughing and chatting with his business partners, playing the big guy, when his smirk suddenly froze as he spotted me coming towards him. I wanted to draw my gun, but knew that would be a reason for suspension, so instead I simply approached him, raised my fist, and planted it in his face.

"You bastard!" I yelled, and stood over him, ready to punch again.

My punch had split his lip and he was bleeding.

"Was it good, huh? Did you enjoy fucking my wife?"

Steven Williams stared at me and at my fist, terrified I would hit him again. But I'd never hit a man who was lying down.

"Just tell me you at least loved her," I said, and stared into his face to see if I could detect any kind of emotion besides fear.

But there was none. He had never loved Arianna. He had used her.

"Where did you do it, huh? Did you take her to a motel, huh? Some sleazy place where you could pay per the hour?"

Steven Williams shook his head.

"Then, where? Tell me. I want to know." I lifted the fist higher and more threateningly in the air. Steven Williams whimpered.

"What was that? I didn't hear you properly."

"At yyyour place. We met at your apartment!"

44

January 2015

I let him go. He wasn't even worth my anger. I drove back to the station, then walked to my office, where I closed the door and sat down. I hid my face in my hands. A picture of Arianna showed up on my laptop. She was holding the twins in her arms, smiling. One of the good days, when she was happy with her family, happy with me. Now I started to doubt everything about our relationship. Had it all just been an act? Had I been betrayed all this time? Why had I even kept the picture? I didn't know. Maybe I still loved her. Maybe I had still hoped, till this day, that she would suddenly change her mind and come back. Maybe I had clung to that hope and thought that if just…if she just had time and space, then she would remember what she had loved about our life; she would come back, at least for the children.

"Why do you keep hurting me, Arianna?" I asked the empty room. "Even when you're not here? Were you ever happy with us?"

They had sex at your place! You fool! They slept together in your apartment, your furniture, your bed. How could you not have known this? How did you not see it? How did you not smell it on her?

There was a knock and Joel Hall peeked inside. "Hey

there. Is everything all right?" he asked. "You look a little pale."

I nodded. "It will be. Some day. What's up?"

He stepped in. "I just wanted to talk to you about those books. The Platt books?" he said.

"Oh, yeah, come on in."

"I talked to some linguistic-experts and had them take a close look at the books, and I'm afraid they agree with Tracey Burden."

"Really?"

"Yes. They say John Platt's language changed drastically three books ago," Joe Hall said.

I leaned back in my chair. "I'll be…"

"They can't say he didn't write them, since they are very similar in style, but especially the last one, the one that was published three months ago, that the family claims they found on his computer by coincidence, is very different. I wrote it all in this report. I thought you might want to take a look at it."

"Thanks," I said, and grabbed the file as Joel Hall left. I read it thoroughly, wondering what this could mean. Had someone else written the books? Maybe the son? Or, could it be…?

I had a feeling, a hunch, but needed more than that, so I grabbed the phone and called for Peter Walker to come in for some questioning. He was sleeping, he told me, after a night shift, but would be able to make it in around noon. I accepted that and hung up. Then I found the files from the killing of the judge on my computer and went through the details once again. I kept returning to the interview with Melanie Schultz's friends and the details about that guy from Animal Control. Where was he? Why couldn't we find him? Animal Control said they didn't know him. Who was he?

I knew it was a high-priority case, and my superiors were screaming for results they could present to the press. The story was still all over the media, who hadn't taken long to figure out exactly what the good judge was doing at Melanie

Schultz's house. Meanwhile, the husband, John Schultz, who had been named the true victim in this case, was being interviewed over and over again, asking the question we all wondered about.

"Where are my wife and son? Where are Melanie and Sebastian?"

The whole story stank of betrayal, just like my own life did.

45

January 2015

I placed two books in front of Peter Walker.

"What am I looking at here?" he asked.

"Two books that are supposed to be written by your father."

"I can see that much. But why am I looking at them?" he asked. He looked at his watch.

"Busy?" I asked. "I thought you worked the night shift."

"I have a life outside of work too," Peter answered.

"I'll make this short, then," I said. I leaned over my desk and pointed at the books. "Here's my little theory. I don't think these two books were written by the same author. And I think you know it. I think your sister Laura had her neighbor from across the street, Rhonda Harris, write three books for her, pretending they were written by John Platt. I think you noticed right away when you read the first book and you confronted your sister about it. Then, I think she offered you money to shut up about it. I think that's why you were there on the night of her murder. You wanted more money. I think Rhonda Harris believed their scam would be revealed once Laura Bennett was killed, and therefore, she killed herself. To not have to live with the shame." I paused for effect. Peter tightened his lips. That's when I knew I was on to the right path. "Am I right?"

Peter Walker looked at me for a long time without speaking. His hands were shaking and he tried to hide them.

"Take your time." I slurped my coffee while Peter fought within himself to determine whether to lie to me or tell the truth. Finally, he opened his mouth. He exhaled.

"All right. But...I...I...I didn't come up with the idea. Laura did. I spotted it right away when I read the first one. There was no way my dad had written that. I confronted her and told her I would reveal it. That she was an imposter and everyone would know. She begged me not to, then offered me money to shut up. I took it. I didn't want my family's name getting dirty either."

"Plus, you could really use the money. With the lifestyle you had been used to growing up, living in a small condo in Cape Canaveral and working the night shift at Ron Jon's wasn't exactly attractive to you."

Peter stared at me. "So, am I in trouble?" he asked.

"That's not for me to decide. I'm in homicide; I usually don't deal with fraud or extortion. But, tell me one thing. Why did Laura Bennett do this? She had enough money, didn't she?"

Peter shook his head. "She made a series of very bad investments. Plus, they were spending like crazy. She needed more money. They say it's the worst thing that can happen to anyone. To suddenly get money. It's like those lottery winners who take home three hundred million, and then two years later they tell the media they are now in debt up to their ears and that winning the money was the worst thing that could have happened to them. Laura and Brandon were like that. They had no idea what they were doing, and she fell for one scam after another. Like I said, I didn't come up with the idea. She did. Laura did. She knew her neighbor across the street wanted to write and made a deal with her. I had nothing to do with it."

No, you only blackmailed them. No harm in that, right?

God, how I loathed sleaze-balls like this guy. So busy

washing his hands afterwards, thinking he didn't do anything wrong.

"What about Brandon Bennett? Was he in on it as well?" I asked.

"No. She was afraid he might find out, and I used that against her. Told her I would tell him if she didn't pay up. It worked."

"How wonderful for you." I cleared my throat. "So, tell me. Did you get angry with her for not wanting to pay up?"

Peter Walker smiled. "I know where you're going with this, Detective."

No shit, Sherlock.

"No, I didn't get angry with her, and I didn't kill her. Why would I? First of all, she did promise me more money that night; second of all, it would be stupid of me to kill the hand that feeds me, don't you think?"

He made a strong point. I let him off the hook for now. None of this indicated that he had killed his sister, and that was all I cared about right now. Somewhere out there in my town, someone would be getting away with murder if I didn't get a breakthrough in this case soon.

Part Two

I'D HAVE TO PACK MY THINGS AND GO

46

February 2015

"Welcome to Motel Albert, a historic Cocoa Beach hotel."

The man behind the counter was tall and well-muscled, even though he did have a little stomach poking out. His hair was brown, but had been lightened by the sun. His skin was tanned, his eyes gentle and blue. He was wearing shorts and a blue T-shirt that was tight over his chest and showed his muscles. It had stains on it, looked like tomato sauce, but could have been something else. He wasn't shaved. He looked like one of those surfers Shannon had seen out the window of her rental car driving through Cocoa Beach. They were everywhere with their long blond messy hair, riding their skateboards, some even while carrying surfboards under their arms. Next to him stood an old woman. Shannon pulled her daughter closer and pulled her hoodie over her head.

"No, Mom. It's too hot," Angela proclaimed angrily and pulled it off.

Shannon growled and pulled it back on. "Just leave it on, okay?"

"Name?" the man behind the counter asked.

Shannon looked around the lobby. It wasn't quite the type

of hotel she was used to staying in, but that was the entire point to it all.

The man behind the counter stared at her, waiting for her reply.

Don't let him see your eyes. Don't let him see your face.

"Name?" she repeated. "Well…Schmidt. I have a reservation booked under the name Schmidt."

"Schmidt, yes," the man said. He turned and pulled out a key. "If you'll just sign here."

He pointed at a piece of paper and Shannon signed it using the alias.

"Okay," the man said and put the paper away without looking at her signature. "Mrs. Schmidt. You'll be in number one-fifteen. Has a nice view of the beach, that one." He handed her the key, then walked around the counter. "My name is Jack. My parents own this place. I help out on the weekends. Let me help you with your suitcases."

"There's no need to," Shannon said, and grabbed the suitcases herself. She turned her head to make sure he didn't see her face, even though it was covered by her scarf. Joe had provided a very rough beating the day before and Shannon was determined this was his last.

Never again.

Angela smiled and stuck out her hand to shake his. "Hello there, Mr. Jack," she said with a grin. "I'm Angela. I am six years old. You can take my suitcase if you like."

"Angela…" Shannon said. "There's really no need to…"

"Ah, but I don't mind," Jack said. "Let me carry it for the young lady. It's right up on the second floor to the right."

Shannon and Angela followed Jack up the stairs and down the long carpeted corridors. He stopped in front of a door, then opened it with the key. It was an old fashioned key, not a card like other hotels had. Everything about this motel was old and seemed like it hadn't been updated since the seventies.

"Here you go," Jack said, and let them inside.

"Thank you," Shannon said, hoping he would leave them alone. She found a twenty-dollar bill and handed it to him.

He chuckled and shook his head. "No need for that."

"Please, I insist," she said. "I'd also appreciate my privacy while I'm here, if you understand."

Jack took the bill, then put it in his pocket. "I'll put this in the tip jar in the bar then. They work hard for their tips down there."

"Whatever," Shannon said.

Jack stayed in the doorway. Shannon wondered why he didn't just leave. He didn't seem like a bellboy, but a lot in this place wasn't like in other hotels. Shannon, who was used to a life of extreme luxury, couldn't remember ever staying in a place like this. Not that it wasn't nice; it was. The dark wood everywhere made it a little somber, though. The floors creaked when she walked on them. The carpets were nice and soft and the beds neatly made. The view was spectacular… sandy beach as far as the eye could see. And the almost green ocean right outside her window. There was a small balcony she could sit on. There were chairs to sit in everywhere, especially on the wooden deck. There didn't seem to be many guests in the motel, which suited her perfectly. You could say the place was charming in its own way. It wasn't massive and big like the hotels she usually stayed in on her tours.

She looked at Jack, wondering why he was still there.

"I'm supposed to tell you about the place. There's a story of a house-ghost that wanders the hallways at night. The story goes she killed herself in one of the rooms downstairs. She was last seen in the bar at the restaurant downstairs. They say she likes to move things around in there."

Jack looked at Angela, like he wondered if those stories would frighten her.

"Don't worry about her," Shannon said. "She loves creepy stuff like that. She has loads of imaginary friends herself. Some of them are dead, she says."

"Have you seen any ghosts?" Angela asked.

Jack chuckled and shook his head. "Not yet. I have two children the same age as you. They're down at the beach now playing with their granddad if you want to come down later?"

Angela made a joyful shriek. Shannon shook her head and saw the disappointment in her daughter's face. But she couldn't be too careful. She had chosen this place because no one would find her here. They wouldn't even think of looking for her here. That would buy her time. Time to figure out... things. Time to find out what she was going to do. If she had to stay in the motel for months before she figured out what to do, then so be it.

"I see you brought a guitar?" Jack asked. "You play?"

"I get by," Shannon said, sensing he was getting a little too nosy now. "Now, if you'll excuse me, we need to get settled in."

"Yes, yes of course. I'm sorry. I didn't mean to impose. I just always wanted to learn how to play. Must be great to have music in your life."

Shannon scoffed. Music was her entire life, and had been for as long as she could remember. It was still her passion, even though it had also made her life complicated over the years, and sometimes she wished she could go back to the time when music was just something she did for fun.

"Anyway," Jack said. He paused and looked at her. "Mrs. Schmidt, I'll see you around. Let me know if there is anything you need. If you have any questions, I'll be glad to be of assistance. I'm here all weekend helping out. I live in a condo right next door. My parents are here 24-7, in case you need anything."

He looked at Angela and reached out his hand. "It was a pleasure to meet you, Angela. I'm sure you and your mom are going to have a great time here at Motel Albert."

He made a funny face and Angela laughed. Shannon smiled, but hid it behind her scarf. He seemed like a nice guy. Not the type to alert the media if he found out who she was, but she could not be too careful.

"The restaurant is always open," he said, looking at Shannon. He had a nice smile.

"I prefer room service," she said.

"That, we don't do. I'm sorry."

"All right. I need to find a pharmacy. Where is the closest?" she asked.

"Right up A1A on the other side of downtown Cocoa Beach."

"Great. Thank you."

"It might be a small town, but they have everything here. We also arrange guided tours, in case you'd like to see what the city has to offer. I bet you'd want to see Kennedy Space Center and maybe take one of the boat rides to see alligators and manatees."

"Alligators!" Angela exclaimed. "I wanna go, Mom. Can we, please?"

"Let's look into it," Shannon said, to keep her daughter from begging more. Truth was, Shannon had hoped they could stay in the room for most of the time, but she knew it would be impossible.

"You can read all about it in our folders in the lobby," Jack said. "There's a lot to choose from. And there are also trips to Disney and SeaWorld in Orlando, of course. Anyway. Welcome."

"Thank you."

47

February 2015

I couldn't believe a month had passed and I was still not closer to cracking any of the cases. I had interrogated Brandon Bennett over and over again, but he still didn't remember much from that night. I was getting nowhere.

I had gone through the Bennett's entire social circle, but no one had a motive, and all had alibis that checked out fine. Including both of her sisters, who were also deprived of their inheritance.

The case of Rhonda Harris's suicide was closed, so that was some good news. But it wasn't good enough. By far. The worst part was the judge. I couldn't believe I had gotten nowhere on his case. I had interviewed tons of criminals that he put away, his family, his political opponents, and still it led me nowhere.

It was driving me crazy.

My dad hadn't been well lately. Not after a bad case of the flu hit him at the end of January. So, I was trying to help out a lot more at the motel. This weekend, I was taking care of everything, so my mom could rest a little as well. It wasn't very busy, so I took my time with the guests and hung out on the deck with some of the snowbirds, telling them where it would be best to fish and where to go to see dolphins. The motel was located on the thinnest part of the barrier island,

and we had water on both sides. They could just cross the road to get to the Intracoastal where they could see manatees and tons of stingrays and dolphins. I really enjoyed hanging out at the motel and realized why my dad had wanted this his entire life. People who came here were happy and cheerful. They were looking to have a great time and enjoy the area, and I got to help them with that. It was so much more rewarding than chasing down a killer, I thought.

I had just shown a new guest to her room, when I went down to the beach to find my kids and tell them it was time for lunch. They were building a humongous sandcastle with their granddad. He was smiling from ear to ear.

"Hey, Son," he said and patted me on the shoulder. "Pretty impressive, huh?"

I chuckled. "I bet I could build one that was bigger," I said, teasing. "But decent work there, Dad. The twins need to eat, though. Grandma is serving mahi-mahi burgers on the deck."

The twins looked at each other, then sprang towards the motel with loud shrieks. Emily was sitting on a towel, listening to music on her phone.

"Aren't you warm in all those black clothes?" My dad asked.

Emily shrugged without looking up. That was her answer to everything lately. It was getting worse. She was shutting all of us out. It made me worry about her.

"Let's eat," I said. "Are you coming?"

"I'm not hungry."

"Come on," I said. "Grandma made mahi-mahi burgers?"

"I don't eat anything with eyes," she said.

That was a new one.

"Since when?" I asked.

"Since now. I just watched a video about how they treat animals. It's cruel, Jack. I don't want to be a part of it. You can't make me."

She was looking for a fight. I wasn't. I shrugged. "Well,

just eat the bread and the lettuce then. Come on. They're all waiting."

"I'll pass," she said.

I felt a pinch in my heart. I hated when she shut me out and when she refused to be a part of the family. "Come on," I said again. "Grandma is going to be so sad if you don't come."

Emily looked up at me. "She's not my grandmother and you know it. Don't pretend it's something when it's not."

"Ouch," I said. I pretended to have been shot. "That. Hurt. Must. Have. Burger. To. Survive."

Emily rolled her eyes at me, but I detected a small smile on her lips as well. Finally, with a deep sigh, she decided to come with me.

48

May 1998

Life without money wasn't a lot of fun, Annie soon realized. Eight years after they had said goodbye to the wealth of Victor's family, she found herself sitting in a small two-bedroom condo in a bad part of town. Her son was now a teenager and she loathed him more than ever. Everything about him made her skin crawl. His eyes, the way he looked, the way he spoke. Everything. When he came home from school, she always hoped he would walk straight into his room without a word and play his computer games. She didn't care what he did in there, in his room, as long as he didn't bother her.

Victor hadn't become more attractive in her eyes either. He no longer wore those expensive suits that he used to, nor did he drive a big car. He had lost everything that was just the slightest bit appealing to her. Annie hated every day of her life, and every day when Victor went off to work and the boy was in school she sat at home and watched soaps, eating ice cream and chocolate, feeling sorry for herself that her life had ended up such a mess. She hated having to clean the house on her own now and do the grocery shopping, and all the laundry piling up every day. It just wasn't the life she had pictured for herself growing up. Not at all.

"It's just all wrong," she said to herself.

But she didn't know what to do to change things around. How to get out of this life. She had no money, and even if she got a divorce, she wasn't even getting any. Still, she couldn't stand this condo, nor could she stand her husband or her son. It was all just miserable.

One day, there was a knock on her front door, and outside stood a detective. He was tall and handsome. He even still had most of his hair, she noticed, when he lifted his cap with a "Ma'am" and showed her his badge.

Annie smiled. It had been years since she had looked at a man and thought he was attractive. Not since Tim, and that didn't end well. She suddenly felt self-conscious in her sweats and carrying the extra weight.

"Yes? What can I do for you, Officer?"

He smiled. "Well, I'm here because I have to ask you some questions. "You are Annie Greenfield, right?"

She shook her head. "I used to be. Now I'm married. Come on in."

Annie let the man in, then excused herself and ran into her bedroom to change. She found a pair of jeans that she couldn't fit into anymore, then found a pair of nice black pants that fit her nicely still, and a purple shirt to go with them. She took her hair down, brushed it and put on some make-up, then returned to the living room, where the detective sat on the couch. His face lit up when he saw her.

"Now. What do you say I make us some coffee?" she asked.

"That sounds really nice."

She ran to the kitchen and came back with coffee and cookies. She placed it all on the table, then sat down across from him.

"So, what did you want to question me about?"

The detective cleared his throat, then opened a file he pulled out of his briefcase. Annie touched a lock of her hair and blushed when he looked at her.

"Well, you see. It's an old matter, but it has come to our attention that back in the mid-eighties there were some students at SFU who used the date rape drug Rohypnol to rape girls. We believe you might be one of their victims. The drug was fairly new back then, so it wasn't something that there was a focus on, but there is now. A man we recently arrested on another rape charge told us you were one of his victims back then."

"Tim?" Annie's voice shivered at the awful memories coming back to her. Images from the night by the lake kept flashing before her eyes.

"Yes. Tim Harrold. He's been arrested in another case here in my district, but he admitted to this as well. We're looking for witnesses. Would you be willing to testify, if it came to it? I would need you to tell me your entire story."

Many thoughts flowed through Annie's mind. Pictures of that terrible night so many years ago, the anger that led to her resentment of her own son, the anger that led her to hate all men. Well, most men. Not the handsome detective. It all made sense. That was why she couldn't remember much from what happened. She had heard about this drug numerous times, but never made the connection. It spiked the anger in her once again. She was tired of being the victim.

"Yes," she said. "I would be delighted to."

49

February 2015

Officer Mike Wagner had been on patrol for three hours. The Cocoa Beach Police Department's car was messy. Mike hadn't cleaned it. He knew he would have to soon, but he hadn't bothered yet.

He opened the window and pulled out a cigar from the pocket of his shirt. He lit it and blew out smoke while looking at the house next to him. He had parked the car on the side of A1A, where the road split into two. He didn't really want to go after people speeding, but hoped they would slow down when they saw him. Officer Mike smoked his cigar. It made him look like Winston Churchill, his colleagues often said. He liked that. Mike had always felt like a big man. Even though he lived in a town where nothing much happened, he still felt important. His work was important. He kept the population safe and was very well-liked among his citizens. As Sergeant, he kept track of all the young kids coming to the force and made sure they understood that they were here to serve the people, not to get off on some big power trip or ego that they might have.

A car drove past him speeding excessively. Officer Mike sighed. He couldn't let that go. The cigar ended in the ashtray and he drove onto the road, soon catching up to the white SUV. He put the siren on and the car slowed down, then stopped. Officer Mike exited his car and walked with big heavy steps up to the SUV. The dreaded walk. He hated the walk. You never knew who might be in the car you had just pulled over. You never knew how they would react to being stopped. Did they have a gun in the car? A colleague of Mike's in Melbourne was shot, not even two months ago, when stopping a speeding car.

You never knew.

Mike spotted the hands on the wheel and noticed they belonged to a woman. That made him relax a little. He usually didn't have anything to fear. Not out on the barrier island, where everything was calm and people usually were respectable. Cocoa Beach was a sleepy town, but had many tourists coming from all over. Mike was always on alert.

"Do you know why I stopped you today, Ma'am?" he asked, as he approached the window. The woman was wearing a hat and sunglasses and a scarf covering her face.

Mike looked inside the car and spotted a young girl in the back seat. His shoulders came down. Nothing but a mom in a hurry.

"No, Officer, I don't," she said.

"You were speeding, Ma'am. A lot."

"I'm sorry, Officer." The woman seemed in distress. "License and registration, please."

The woman leaned over and opened the glove compartment. When she returned and handed him the papers, the scarf fell down and revealed big bruises. It bothered Officer Mike. There were few things that could make him really angry, but a wife beater was one of them.

He looked at the driver's license. Then he froze, immediately star struck.

Shannon King, the famous country singer!

He could hardly speak. His lips were trembling. "I'm sorry, Miss King. I didn't know it was you. Are you having a concert nearby, or…?"

She shook her head and re-covered her face with the scarf.

"No. I'm visiting. I would appreciate keeping my visit private, though. If possible, Officer?"

Mike nodded and handed her back her driver's license. He pulled out his notepad. "Naturally. Do you mind?" he said. "I'm a big fan."

Shannon King sighed, then grabbed the pad and pen. She signed it and handed it back.

"Was that all, Officer? I need to get to the pharmacy."

"Well, of course. Just remember, only 35 here on this part of A1A."

"I must have missed the sign. I'm sorry, Officer."

"No problem, Miss King. We're happy to have you in town. May I ask what brings you here?"

"I'm visiting some old friends. Trying to stay away from the media, though. So, if you'd please…"

"Naturally, Ma'am. My lips are sealed. Enjoy your stay."

50

February 2015

"I MISS MOMMY!"

The Snakecharmer looked at his son, then slapped him across the face. "Don't say that, Son. She was nothing but a cheating bitch. All women are!"

"Leave the kid alone." The Snakecharmer's dad sat across from him at the kitchen table. "It's not his fault. You just stay away from women, Son. You hear me?"

"Y-yes, Grandpa," the kid whimpered, then ran to his room.

"Now, what are you planning on doing with that one over there?" his dad asked, as he nodded towards Will in the playpen.

The Snakecharmer drank from his beer. "I don't know."

"Don't you think people will start asking questions at some point?"

"I just couldn't leave him there, you know?" The Snakecharmer said, and looked at the kid. He liked him.

"Well, you should have. Kids are trouble. Where did you find him anyway?"

The Snakecharmer looked at the TV in the corner. Luckily, it didn't work. His dad couldn't see anything anyway, but he might hear something. Fortunately, he never left the house, so there was no way he would ever know where the kid had come from. Even though his picture was everywhere.

"I told you. I found him in a dumpster behind the Publix grocery store."

His dad grunted. "You should have given him to the cops. Now we're stuck with him."

"They would just put him in some foster home, and what good would that do him? I like the kid. I can raise him right."

"Don't you think you've got enough on your plate with that one in there?" he said.

"I'll manage. I got it covered, Dad, don't worry."

The Snakecharmer had gotten rid of Melanie. She hadn't lasted more than a week before the smell became too bad. It annoyed him. The Snakecharmer was starting to miss the action. He knew the ground was burning underneath him, but still he felt an itch, a strong desire pulling him. He wanted more. He had already spotted his next victim, and visited her last month down in Satellite Beach. He had kept an eye on her for weeks now and knew her everyday routine to the smallest detail. That was the way he worked. Stayed in complete control. Murderers were caught because they made mistakes. Because they got too eager or thought they were safe; they got stupid or suddenly impulsive. He wasn't going to do that. He was smarter than any of them, and he was going to show them.

"What's wrong, Son?" His dad asked.

The Snakecharmer drank his beer. "Nothing's wrong."

"You seem so tense lately."

The Snakecharmer finished his beer, then went to the fridge and got himself another one. "I just need to get laid. It's been awhile."

His dad laughed. "Yeah, well, as long as you don't marry them. That's when trouble begins."

"I know," he said and thought about his ex-wife. The bitch had been seeing someone else. He had smelled it on her and asked her, but, oh no, it was just from hugging one of her friends. Yeah, right. As soon as he suspected something was going on, he had followed her. And, sure enough. He had seen her with another man. He had been all over her.

Lying, cheating bitch.

51

February 2015

The following Monday, I had a small breakthrough in the case of Laura Bennett. For weeks, I had gone through old cases of women being killed in the area, and suddenly I found one that caught my attention.

A young girl of only seventeen had been killed thirteen years ago, in 2002, in her own home in Melbourne Beach. Her parents had been out with friends, and when they returned they found the daughter on the floor, strangled to death. The case was considered a breaking and entering and it was believed she must have surprised the burglar with the result that he killed her in a panic.

It all seemed like the right conclusion, given the evidence. There had been stolen jewelry and a window in the back had been forced open, and there were visible marks from the use of a crowbar. There was just one thing that didn't add up.

The ME had concluded that she had been washed afterwards.

I couldn't believe it. The police report concluded she had to have been taking a shower before the burglar broke into her house, even though it clearly stated in the ME's autopsy report that she had been washed after death had occurred. Washed with bleach.

Just like they had in the case of Laura Bennett.

I called Sheriff Ron and told him what I had found, and then went to Weasel's office to tell her as well.

"I'll be..." she said. "So, you're telling me this is not his first?"

"That's what I'm saying."

"But, in that case, he used his hands and not a pillow?" she asked.

"He learned from his mistakes. He was younger back then and less careful. It might have been his first kill. He doesn't want to bruise the body, especially not the face. That's why he uses the pillow now."

"Good work, Detective," Weasel said. "I'm impressed."

After work, I drove to my parents' motel, feeling a little better for once. I wasn't closer to catching this guy, but now I was getting to know him a little. All I needed was for him to make a mistake.

"They all do at some point," the chief of my old homicide unit in Miami used to say to me. I was hoping he was right.

I parked the Jeep outside the motel, then walked up to the deck where I found Abigail and Austin playing with the little girl Angela. They had been hanging out all weekend, even though I got the feeling the mother wasn't too fond of her doing so. I took it she was just one of those overly protective women, but I knew something else was going on. The way she kept covering her face told a different story. I had seen it a lot of times before, and it pissed me off every time.

"They play well together, don't they?" Mrs. Schmidt had walked up behind me and stopped.

"They really do. It's been awhile since my twins played like this without fighting," I said, and looked at the woman next to me. She was attractive. Everyone could tell she was somebody, even though she covered her face with a scarf and wore sunglasses all the time. It was in the way she moved. She constantly attracted her surroundings' attention, even though she didn't want to. People simply couldn't take their eyes off of her. I couldn't blame them. I felt the same way.

"So, when are you going to tell me your real name?" I asked.

The woman looked at me. "I'm sorry, what?"

"I don't know why you have a made-up reservation in a false name, and it's none of my business," I said. "But, Mrs. Schmidt?"

She chuckled. "I guess it was a little thick."

"It's okay with me if you want to hide. I'm a detective around here. I can keep a secret."

She nodded. I sensed she blushed underneath the scarf. "Well, okay then, Detective Ryder. You can call me Shannon."

I turned and shook her hand. She took off her sunglasses and looked me in the eye. That was when I realized who she was, and understood why she had to hide herself. It took me quite by surprise.

"Nice to meet you, Shannon."

52

February 2015

Officer Mike Wagner's shift was almost over, and he sat at the station eating his sandwich with one of his colleagues, John.

"So, how was your shift?" John asked.

Mike took another bite and chewed, then shrugged. "Quiet, as usual."

Some of the guys were playing darts at the other end of the room and were cheering loudly.

"Had a couple of speeding mamas and a drunk hobo annoying the tourists on the beach."

"I hate the hobos," John said, and drank from his Big Gulp. "Especially the drunk ones."

"I know. It's Friday, so there will be lots of teenagers on the beach tonight drinking and making bonfires. Make sure they don't burn stuff that isn't theirs, if you know what I mean."

He swallowed the last bite of his sandwich. He could have waited till he got back to the condo to eat, but he liked to have the company. He would probably still munch on a bag of chips in the recliner while watching CSI, once he got home. He needed to grocery shop, but didn't feel like it today. He still had enough chips and sodas for a couple of days. He'd get by. Then he'd hit Wal-Mart at the beginning of next week.

"Working next weekend, I hear?" John said.

"Yes," Mike said. "Both days. But, it's all good. I like work."

John chuckled. "I'd rather be home with the wife and kiddos."

Mike nodded. He didn't want to talk about other people's families. He didn't like to hear about them or how happy they were. He had never had a family of his own and after reaching forty, he had stopped thinking it would come. Not that he hadn't had girlfriends, he did, but they never wanted him long enough. They all split after just a few weeks. He'd never quite figured out why.

"Say, what's that on your notepad?" John asked.

Mike looked at the table where he had put his things down. His phone, his radio, and his notepad.

His notepad with Shannon King's autograph!

"Does it say Shannon King?" John asked, and pulled it to better see.

Mike put a hand to cover it. "Leave it," he said.

"How did you get Shannon King's autograph? John asked loudly. Too loudly. Now the dart-playing colleagues turned to look.

"What's going on here?" George said, approaching them.

"Tell them, Sergeant," John said. "Tell us how you got Shannon King's autograph?"

"What?" George said. "The singer? Damn, she's hot. You meet her somewhere?"

Mike still didn't answer. "Come on, guys," he said. "It's private."

"She's here, isn't she?" John asked with a grin. "Oh, my God. Shannon King is in Cocoa Beach!"

"Is it true, Sergeant?" George said. "Come on, tell us."

Mike sighed. How was he supposed to lie to his buddies? He couldn't. They were his family, his friends, and his entire life. Besides, he really wanted to tell someone about his meeting with the most famous country singer on the planet.

"Yes," he said. "Yes, she was here. I pulled her over for

speeding. She had her daughter with her. So, I asked for her autograph."

His colleagues burst into a loud roar. Mike got up, trying to leave. He'd said too much. It made him feel bad.

"Hey, wait a minute there, tiger," George said. "Tell us some more. What did she look like in real life? She is gorgeous, isn't she? What is she doing in Cocoa Beach? Did she have bodyguards with her or anything?"

Mike shook his head. "No. It was just her and the kid. And she told me she wanted this to stay private. She wanted to keep it a secret from the press. And, we keep it that way, you hear me?"

"She can't keep that a secret for long," John said. "Someone will see her and tell the press."

Mike looked at his boys. John was right. The place would soon be crawling with journalists looking for her.

"That might be, but it won't come from any of us, you hear me?"

John saluted him with a grin. "Loud and clear, Sir!"

53

February 2015

Happy hour oysters are back!

I put the small sign up outside of the restaurant like my mom had asked me to. Today's special was Mahi-Mahi and Grouper, she had written in chalk on the small blackboard.

That was the special every day, it seemed.

The kids had been playing so well, I had been able to go surfing for an hour. When I got back out of the water, I felt refreshed and new and helped my mother change the menu before the guests arrived for dinner...the few of them that chose to eat at the motel. It had actually been a slow winter for my parents, and as we were getting closer to the spring, it had my mother worried. Even though she tried to hide it.

"It'll pick up," she kept saying. "Snowbirds will come. They always do."

But the season for snowbirds was almost over. My dad's health still wasn't too well, and he needed a lot of rest. There was another chance. Springer-breakers came in March, and even though they were often loud and caused trouble with their excessive drinking, they meant business. They liked to stay in cheap motels on the beach.

I helped my mother cook for the guests and for our family. I made a salad for Emily, who had been very into eating healthy lately, and I didn't want to discourage her from that, even though my mother thought it was nonsense.

"Who doesn't like meat?"

"Just let her be herself. She's trying to figure out who she is, and we should let her," I said.

We served burgers for everyone—except Emily—and sat down to eat all together. I loved these family dinners. We even had two extras sitting with us today, since Shannon King and Angela had agreed to have dinner with us. I really liked her, so I hoped we would all be on our best behavior.

It was a success, and while the kids ran onto the beach afterwards, playing ball, Shannon and I took a stroll with our feet in the water. I pointed out a pod of dolphins for her that were playing in the waves and she gasped in awe.

"I see them all the time out there, when I surf," I said.

"That sounds amazing," she said. "You have quite the life here, Detective. A true paradise."

"Maybe I should teach you how to surf while you're here?" I asked.

Shannon chuckled. "Me? Oh no. I'm not cut out for that. Water isn't my thing. Give me a horse and I can show you a trick or two."

I laughed. "I forgot. You're from Texas."

She laughed lightly. It felt good to walk with her. I enjoyed spending time with her, but I also knew she was married. She never talked about her husband, but she didn't have to.

"So, did he do that to you?" I asked, and pointed at her face where the scarf had fallen down slightly on the side and a bruise showed.

She went quiet.

I went too far.

Then, she nodded. "I had to get away. Mostly for Angela's sake. She started to ask questions. I can't let her grow up like this."

I exhaled, then reached out a hand and touched her bruise gently. I hated men who beat their wives more than anything

I could think of. Only cowards would do such a thing. I had seen so much of this when living in Miami.

She grabbed my wrist and held on to it. She looked me in the eyes. I held my breath. I hadn't felt like this for a very long time.

"I..." she said. She removed her eyes from mine. "I should go."

She turned around and went back to the motel.

I stared after her, feeling frustrated. I couldn't fall for this woman. Could I? No, she was too complicated. She was married. She was a celebrity. It couldn't be. I had just met her. No, it was just a crush. It was nothing, I told myself. But I knew I was wrong.

I was already in deep…in over my head.

54

February 2015

S hannon rushed back to the room, holding her phone in her hand. She found the key and locked herself in. She ran to the balcony, where she could see Angela playing on the beach with the twins. She could see Jack. He was still standing on the beach where she had left him.

This isn't good, Shannon.

She couldn't fall for him. This was no time to start a romance. She felt so frustrated. She really liked the guy and they had just shared something. Was that a moment? Had they shared something on the beach just now?

No, she couldn't let anyone into her life now. Not the way it was.

She looked at the display on her phone. Her manager, Bruce, had called and left a message. He was the only one who knew this number. She hadn't told him where she was going, only that he could reach her at this number in case it was important. She listened to the message.

"Joe is looking everywhere for you, Shannon," he said. "He was here earlier this morning, trying to force me to tell him where you were. I told him you had left...that you weren't coming back. He went crazy. He trashed the mirror in my hallway, you know the beautiful one you love so much.

He's angry. Stay hidden and stay safe. Don't let anyone know where you are. Not until we get the restraining order through. Shit, he scared me. He wants Angela, he said. Please don't take your eyes off of her, promise me that. Well, I gotta go. I hope y'all are still safe. Don't worry about the press. I got it covered, and I managed to cancel the rest of your tour. I told them you were sick. They will start to ask questions soon, though, so we need to figure out what to tell them."

Shannon put the phone down with a sigh, then went to the window and spotted Angela again. She was still playing with Jack's kids. They had been so sweet to Angela. Shannon found an old address book and a number. She stared at the number for a long time before she found the courage to call it.

"Hello?" a woman said.

"Hello. Is this Kristi?" Shannon asked.

"It is. Who am I speaking to?"

Shannon felt tears fill her eyes and tried to hold them back. She choked on her own sobs. "It's me, Kristi. It's Shannon."

Silence for a little while, an awful silence, while Shannon wondered if she had made a mistake, if she should just hang up again. Then there was a shriek.

"Shannon? Is it really you?"

"Yes. It is me," she said, crying.

She could hear Kristi was crying too. "I...I thought I'd never hear from you again."

"I know. I'm sorry. It's all been a little..." she paused and cried. She pulled away the scarf and took off the hat, then looked at herself in the mirror while crying. "It's just been so awful. You know how you want to do everything for your kid, everything you can to make sure she grows up in a real home with a mom and a dad. It's just...life is just not always like in the movies, you know?"

"Oh, dear sis. I'm sorry to hear that. Is it Joe? I had a feeling he was the one keeping you away from us."

"He never thought my family was good enough. And then

there were the drugs, and I couldn't...I couldn't stop it, not until we had Angela."

Kristi was crying heavily at the other end. "I read about your daughter. I always wanted to meet her. I can't believe I've never met my niece."

"I'm so sorry you haven't. You have no idea how many times I've wanted to call you or just drive to Florida to visit you, but I was afraid of how Joe would react. And then you moved all the way to Cocoa Beach. I mean, when you lived in the Panhandle, I felt you were closer; this is just so far away."

"We moved because of Jimmy's job. He works at the Space Center now. He was one of those that survived the layoffs when the shuttle program stopped. We lucked out. Now he's working on the Orion rocket."

"That sounds really good. I'm so glad you guys are happy," Shannon sobbed.

"So, why are you calling all of a sudden?" Kristi asked. "Did something happen?"

"I left him, Kristi. I left Joe."

Saying the words made her cry again. It had been the hardest decision she ever had to make. For years, she had stayed with Joe because she didn't dare to do anything else. For years, he beat the crap out of her whenever he wanted to, so she had to cancel concerts and lie to everyone about how she got her bruises. Before Angela came along, she had taken a lot of drugs just to put up with his abuse, but when she became pregnant, she had stopped. Finally, she had started seeing things clearly and realized she had to leave him. Especially now that Angela was older and suddenly understood what was going on.

"So, where are you now?" Kristi asked. "Do you want me to come up? I can catch a flight out of Orlando later today if you need me to."

Shannon wept again. She hadn't dared to hope that her sister would greet her with open arms after so many years. But, of course she would. They had been so close up until the day she had met Joe and Joe had told her that her sister was jealous of her and that she should stay away.

All those lies. All that deceit.

"You don't need to," Shannon said. "I'm here. I'm in Cocoa Beach."

55

February 2015

H e was disgusted. The Snakecharmer felt nauseated by what he had just seen. He had been observing Detective Ryder from afar, like he often did, and what was that he had seen? Had the dear detective had a moment with another woman?

With a married woman?

He couldn't believe his own eyes. He knew perfectly well who the woman was, even though she did everything she could to keep it a secret. The Snakecharmer knew everything that went on in his town, and when a celebrity showed herself, rumors spread fast. He had always liked the dear Mrs. King's music, but he certainly wasn't going to anymore. Not after what he had just witnessed. She was coming on to another man? When she was still married? How despicable!

The Snakecharmer wondered for a little while what to do next. He was supposed to go to Satellite Beach and make the last arrangements for his abduction of the woman down there, the one he had been planning on taking for a long time. But, now he was suddenly not so sure anymore. A new plan was shaping in his head. One that was suddenly a lot more urgent than the original one.

But, would it work? Would it really work? It had to. Besides, everything he had done lately had been a success. He had punished all these women for their cheating ways. They had paid their dues. He wouldn't be surprised if someday people would be grateful to him. He had, after all, rid the world of some of its worst scum. Once they figured out what he had done, why he had done it, they would understand; they would even applaud him for his accomplishments. Men would praise him all over the world.

Of course they would.

But, for now, he had to settle for being considered a simple murderer. It was okay. Most artists weren't appreciated in their time.

The Snakecharmer chuckled to himself when thinking about the woman Detective Ryder hadn't found out about yet. The Snakecharmer knew he had found out about the girl back in '02. She had been the Snakecharmer's first girlfriend. A lying cheating bitch like the rest of them. He had gotten away with it almost too easily. He still remembered her pale skin and how fragile she had felt when he had washed her to clean off all her impurity. To think she had slept with that Alex-guy from her class. Someone had told the Snakecharmer about it, and he had broken it off with her right away. Pretended he didn't care. He had spent a year planning everything. Making it look like a burglary. He had read how to do that in one of John Platt's books. How ironic, he thought to himself. But because he had waited so long, no one ever thought about him as a suspect in the case, and soon they ruled it out as a breaking and entering gone wrong.

Too easy.

To be fair, the Snakecharmer admitted that he knew that not all women were lying and cheating. Some were good women. They were out there. He had thought Shannon King was one of them. Until today. But that just showed that you never knew.

Even with your own damn wife, you never knew.

Detective Ryder was finally moving up towards the motel now, after the moment. He was walking right towards the

Snakecharmer now. He felt so excited as Detective Ryder came closer and closer.

The detective smiled and nodded. "How are you, Ma'am?"

"Hello, Detective," the Snakecharmer said with a big grin, as Jack Ryder walked past him. He could almost not hold back his resentment. What he had seen repulsed him to a degree where he knew he had to do something to solve this situation. Action had to be taken in this matter. And he knew exactly what to do.

56

February 2015

"What are we doing here, Mom?"

Angela had been asking questions all the way in the car. She had been playing with Jack's twins all morning, and had started whining when Shannon told her they had lunch plans and had to go. "I told you. We're here to see someone Mommy knows. They would like to meet you."

The neighborhood her sister had bought a house in was called Snug Harbor. It was an area located next to the canals and the Intracoastal River on the backside of the barrier island. All the houses were waterfront and had a seawall with docks and boats or jet skis. You could still walk or bike to the beach. It was very nice, Shannon thought to herself.

You did well for yourself in life, dear sister.

"But who lives here?" Angela asked. "Who are these people? Do they have children?"

"No. They don't."

"Aw."

Kristi was Shannon's older sister by three years. She hadn't been able to have children, something she figured out very early in her teens when she accidentally became pregnant and their mother forced her to have an abortion, something Kristi had never forgiven her mother for. The abortion destroyed her ability to become pregnant again, the doctors told her.

Shannon took in a deep breath before she rang the doorbell. Her stomach was tossing and turning, and she was about to turn around and run away several times before the door was opened.

She looks just like I remember her. Older, but still the same.

Tears piled up in her sister's eyes. She cupped her mouth. "Oh, my God, Shannon. Is that really you?"

Shannon swallowed hard, then nodded with a sob.

Kristi's eyes turned to Angela. "And this is…?"

Shannon nodded, still biting her lip to not burst into tears.

Angela reached out her hand. "Hi. I'm Angela. I'm six years old."

Kristi smiled widely, then sobbed heavily. "Oh, my God. It's really you? Well, hello there, Angela. Welcome to our home. We are so happy you're here."

Angela looked at her mother.

"Well, don't stay out there," Kristi said, and grabbed Shannon's arm right where it was bruised.

Shannon pulled back in pain. "Ouch."

"Mommy fell," Angela said. "Hurt her arm and face. She does this all the time. Stupid stairs."

Kristi looked at Shannon with a worried expression. "Well, good thing we don't have stairs in our house, then," she said. "Come on in."

Inside the living room waited Jimmy. He too had tears in his eyes. He had always loved Shannon, and had been the one to tell Kristi she needed to address Shannon's drug abuse before it was too late. He was the one who told Kristi to intervene, to not let go, even when Kristi wanted to because Shannon treated her badly. That was when Joe started to tell Shannon that Kristi and Jimmy were bad for Shannon, that they were jealous and only wanted to hurt her, to destroy her career. Shannon hadn't liked what he said, but she hadn't cared about anyone either. All she had cared about back then was getting her next fix. The drugs had made her a killer performer on stage, no doubt about it, and her record label hadn't tried to stop it. It had made her even more creative in her songwriting, but it had also destroyed her life. She could see that now. And she had missed out on so much.

"It's so good to see you, Shannon," he said and hugged her. She closed her eyes and enjoyed the embrace. This was exactly what she needed right now. Family.

"Hi, I'm Angela, I'm six," Angela said, and reached out her hand.

Jimmy grabbed her in his arms and held her tight. "I'm so happy to meet you, Angela, who is six years old."

"I hope y'all like shrimp," Kristi said, wiping her tears on her sleeve.

57

February 2015

"How hard can it be to find a woman and a child? A world famous woman and her child!"

Joe Harrison was screaming at the top of his lungs. He grabbed a pile of magazines and threw them at the private investigator he had hired to find Shannon and Angela. He had told him to find Shannon, the most famous singer on the face of the Goddamn planet, whose face was plastered on the cover of all of the magazines, but still he came up with nothing?

Even his buddies at the police station hadn't been able to help him. How the hell could this happen?

"Did you try her sister's place?" he asked the PI.

"Yes. She doesn't live there anymore. Neighbors say they moved six years ago, but they don't know where to."

"And her drunk mother?"

"Still lives in the trailer park in St. Pete, but she hasn't seen her or heard from her in years. I spoke to her on the phone earlier," the PI said.

"How can people just vanish?" Joe yelled. "I don't understand. I want her found. I want her found now! Go down there and talk to the old hag. Tell her I'll freaking kill her if she doesn't tell me where her daughter is."

"Yes, Sir," the PI said, then left.

Joe threw himself on the couch. What had she done? He couldn't believe it had come to this. After all they had gone through? How could she just leave him like this? Well, she wasn't getting away with it. That was certain. She wasn't taking Angela from him...that was for sure. He wanted his daughter back, no matter how much it would cost.

Joe hit his fist into the wall and left a hole. It hurt like crazy. He yelled and picked up some African sculpture that Shannon had paid thousands of dollars for. Joe had always believed it was ugly as hell, and now he threw it to the marble tiles and it scattered into bits and pieces. He growled, then fell to his knees and cried, while picking up the pieces.

"How could you do this to me, Shannon? Don't you know I'm nothing without you? Don't you realize I can't live without you and Angela in my life? How could you just leave like this?"

When he picked up a piece of the sculpture, he cut his finger and it started to bleed. Joe stared at the blood as it dripped to the floor. It was as red as the rage inside of him.

There is no way she is going to get away with this. No way.

Joe screamed. It echoed in the empty million dollar house. His phone rang, and he picked it up.

"Yes?"

"It's me. I have news."

Joe got up from the floor with the phone to his ear. "Sergeant. How wonderful to hear from you."

"I heard from colleagues in Florida that Shannon was spotted in Cocoa Beach. You didn't hear it from me. Now we're even," he said and hung up.

"We're even when I say we are," Joe said, and put the phone in his pocket. There were small drops of his blood on the floor. He found a tissue and wiped the blood off of his finger. He approached a framed picture of Shannon from one of her tours.

"So, Cocoa Beach, huh? That's where you're hiding. Well, not for long, my dear. Not for long."

58

February 2015

T om came over Sunday afternoon with his board under his arm. I grinned when I saw him.

"Seriously? She's letting you surf?" I asked.

"I couldn't believe it either," Tom said. He had brought his 9.2 foot yellow Robert August longboard. A sheer beauty for the eye. I had always been jealous of that board and asked him numerous times if he would sell it. I was glad to see that he was going to use it for what it was meant for, and not just as a decoration in his living room.

"Are you coming?" he asked.

"Give me a sec to suit up."

I looked at my mother, who was sweeping the wooden deck. She smiled. "Go ahead. I'll look after the kids."

"Great. Thanks. Emily is watching TV. She can help if there is anything you need," I said, rushing towards my condo next door. In less than two minutes, I had put on my wetsuit and waxed the board. When I came down to the water, Tom had already paddled out. I hurried after him. I paddled out, enjoying the occasional splash of water in my face. It was getting warmer now, ready for spring that was right around the corner, when the suits came off and we surfed in nothing but shorts. I looked forward to that. I hated wearing my suit. I always felt so trapped.

"You hear that Katherine is back?" Tom asked, when I had paddled out to the back where he waited for the next set. A flock of pelicans flew past him. One dove into the ocean and caught fish that it gulped down immediately.

Katherine was a great white shark that liked to roam the East Coast. Usually, she stayed up north in North Carolina or outside Jacksonville, but every now and then, she swam all the way down to the Space Coast. Last year, she had been all the way to the Gulf and then back. On her way, she had been very close to the beach in Sebastian Inlet, just a few miles south of us. She was wearing a tracker, and we followed her on an app. It was mostly for fun. I wasn't scared of any sharks. We saw them constantly in the water, and often very close to our boards, but those were smaller, not great whites like Katherine.

"Yeah, Florida Today wrote about it yesterday. But she's still far out in the Atlantic," I said, and spotted a set coming through in the back. I got ready, paddled, and caught one. It was smooth and beautiful. Open faced almost all the way to the beach. I did a couple of turns and walked to the tip and tried to do a hang-five, but I fell off. I got back up on the board and paddled back out, just as Tom caught a wave, and I watched him ride it. Tom was an excellent surfer. A whole lot better than I was. It was a shame he didn't surf much anymore.

When he came back, the ocean was quiet for a while. I took in a couple of deep breaths of the fresh air. Tom was very quiet. I got a feeling something was wrong.

"Are you all right?" I asked.

"Well…" he paused and looked at me.

Uh-oh. Something was really wrong.

"Is it Eliza?" I asked. I had sensed it when I was there. It wasn't just the secret they had kept from me. There was more under the surface.

"It's me. I've done something stupid, Jack. And now I'm paying for it. I had to tell her. I was so scared."

"Whoa, whoa. Let's start from the beginning here. What did you do?"

Tom couldn't look at me when he spoke. "I slept with someone."

"Oh, no, Tom!"

"Oh, yes. I did." He groaned and clenched his fist. "I didn't mean for it to happen. It just did. I...I...There is no excuse."

I felt angry at him for being so stupid. Thinking about how I had felt when they told me about Arianna's betrayal, I suddenly felt for Eliza. Being deceived by someone you loved, someone you believed loved you back, was the worst feeling in the world.

"Who was she?"

"That's the worst part," Tom said. "That's why I had to tell. I was scared the police would come after me. I was afraid you...you would."

"Me? Is that why you didn't return my calls for days?" I asked, thinking about how I couldn't get ahold of my best friend for several days in January.

"Yes. I avoided you. Eliza thought it was important we told you about Arianna. Since she now knew how bad it felt. That's why she invited you over. She wanted a clean slate. I was afraid of losing you."

I frowned. "So, why were you afraid the police would come after you for sleeping with someone...unless...oh, my God, Tom. Please tell me it isn't true."

Tom nodded. "It's true. And it's bad. I slept with Laura Bennett right before she was killed. I thought you would find my DNA all over her. We used a condom, but still."

The news was so shocking that I let several excellent waves go past me. "We didn't. Her body was washed with bleach, leaving no traces of anything on her. How long before she was killed did you sleep with her?"

"In the afternoon of the night she died," he said. "We met on Sunday afternoon at a motel."

"Oh, my goodness, Tom."

"I know. A cliché. At least we didn't choose your motel. We took the Motel 6."

"Well, thanks a lot. So, I take it you had been seeing each other for awhile, then?" I asked, hoping I wouldn't have to put Tom's picture up on the whiteboard as a suspect.

He nodded without looking at me. "A couple of months."

"Poor Eliza," I said.

"I know. I'm not proud of myself. But we were going through some stuff. I fell in. I met Laura through the school. We both volunteered at the multicultural night six months ago. We planned it all together and talked every day for like a week or so. We liked each other. I thought she was sweet and funny, and really good to talk to. We started meeting up for coffee now and then. I kept running into her everywhere all of a sudden. Then, one day, we kissed when we said goodbye. Right in the middle of Minutemen, where everyone could see us. Luckily, no one did. But we wanted more. We decided to meet at the motel. One meeting led to another, and soon we saw each other regularly. Eliza and I were going through some bad stuff. I was feeling awful; I felt like Eliza had stopped loving me. Then, Laura was suddenly there. She liked me. Laura liked me. We talked about me and Eliza and how hard it was for us. She told me about the excruciating loss of her child, and how Brandon blamed her. How he drank and gambled, and how it was getting worse and worse since their daughter died. We both needed a shoulder to cry on. We connected. We could relate. But soon, one thing led to another. I couldn't stop, even though I wanted to. I hated to hurt Eliza like that, but being with Laura made me feel so good, I couldn't stop."

Tom paused and sighed. "I can't believe she's dead."

"So, you got scared when she was found killed and told Eliza everything?" I asked. "She sent you here today, didn't she? She didn't let you surf. She wanted you to come clean to me."

"She's been telling me to talk to you for weeks. I kept

avoiding it. Especially since I thought you were mad at us for keeping the secret from you."

"You know me. I don't stay angry that long," I said.

"I feel awful. I've destroyed everything. I had to tell her. I didn't want her to learn from the police or the news when I was arrested," he said, his voice breaking. "That would just be cruel."

Yes that would have been cruel. Just like not telling your best friend his wife was cheating on him until four years later. I couldn't believe it. Was everyone cheating on each other these days? Arianna? Tom? Laura Bennett?

A new set of gorgeous waves were rolling towards me, but I didn't notice. A thought had struck me, and it wouldn't leave.

Melanie Schultz had been cheating too.

59

October 1998

She anticipated his visits with great longing. They were the highlight of her entire week. Every Thursday, he had the day off, and that was when he stopped by the condo. It was the happiest time of Annie's life.

She started to dress nicely again. She started wearing make-up and exercising and was quickly losing weight. Victor didn't suspect a thing, but enjoyed this new and joyful Annie. Little did he know, she was dressing nicely and taking care of herself for someone else.

The handsome officer was at her door this Thursday at exactly ten o'clock, like usual. The boy was at the high school, and Victor was working. Since he had lost his job at his parent's company and had to get by on his own, he had started a pool company. He had a shop downtown and visited people's houses and cleaned their pools. Made sure the PH-balance was right and vacuumed them. It was a good job for him. He enjoyed it immensely.

"Lots of fresh air and I'm my own boss," he would say. "Doesn't get much better than that."

But he never made much money. As a matter of fact, they had gotten deep into debt, and creditors called almost every day now. Victor was probably going to lose his shop if things didn't get better.

Annie didn't care one bit about him or what went on with his shop. She wanted out, and now she had found a way. The handsome officer was going to be her way out of this misery. He wasn't rich, but he made a decent living, and he could take proper care of her.

If only he weren't married.

But, then again. So was she. There was a word to solve that. Divorce. She was ready to take that step right now, but she wasn't so sure about him. He seemed more reluctant, and wasn't willing to discuss it with her. She couldn't quite figure him out. He seemed so into her when he was there, but as soon as she brought up the future, he hesitated and didn't want to talk anymore. Annie knew he was going through a rough time at home. They had talked about it, and he often said that he wasn't sure they would make it. Why wasn't he jumping aboard right away? What was he waiting for?

She had considered getting herself pregnant. That way, he would have to choose. But it was a lot of trouble to go through. She had recently lost a lot of weight and looked great. She certainly didn't want to ruin that.

Only if she had to.

She had decided the pregnancy would be her plan B. Plan A was to make him so fond of her, make him love her so much, he would want to marry her and leave that wife of his.

There was a knock on the door and Annie rushed to open it. She stopped at the mirror next to the door and corrected her hair, right before she pulled it open, trying not to seem too eager. There he was. Outside on her doorstep. Looking even more handsome than the last time he was there, it seemed.

"Come on in," she said with a shy smile.

He walked inside and she closed the door. He looked at her with those blue eyes of his. She was breathing heavily now. He turned her on like no other man had ever done. She had never known sex could be like this. Not since Tim Harrold ruined it for her back at the lake fourteen years ago. It was like the officer had opened her eyes. Like she had been asleep all these years, living in a drowsy bubble of nothing-ness, and now she had finally come to life.

He had made her come alive.

Seconds after he came inside, they were deep in each other's arms. Kissing, touching, feeling. He lifted her up and carried her to the couch, where he ripped off her dress in one smooth movement. Seconds later, he was inside of her, on top of her, panting, breathing. She closed her eyes and let herself get into it with him, secretly wishing she would get pregnant, so he had to take care of her, when suddenly there was a noise behind them. She gasped and opened her eyes, and stared directly into those of her teenage son.

60

February 2015

"So, what are you doing tomorrow?" Kristi asked, when Shannon was putting on her jacket and getting ready to leave. It had been a great day and evening. Shannon couldn't believe how much she had missed her sister. They had talked for hours and hours, catching up on everything; they had cried and laughed, and even been quiet just to enjoy each other's company again.

"I...I wasn't planning on much," Shannon said.

"I wanna go see the alligators!" Angela exclaimed.

Kristi lit up. "That's a good idea," she said. "It's Monday. I have the day off. We can go with you. We can take one of the airboat rides into the river. They always find something. We might see manatees too." Kristi looked at her husband. "We can take the one up at Lone Cabbage. Oh, it's wonderful. We could do the Lil' Twister...that's a private tour where you go deeper into St. John's River. We did it once. It was a lot of fun."

"Did you see alligators?" Angela asked.

"Yes. Lots of them."

"You've seen alligators before," Shannon said to Angela. "At the zoo, remember?"

"Yeah, but they were so boring. I want to see them in real life."

"I really don't..." Shannon said. "I can't go anywhere where there are too many people."

Her sister nodded, understanding what she meant. She couldn't be recognized, and she certainly couldn't risk anyone seeing her bruised face.

"I understand," Kristi said. "You know what? Why don't we take her? Let me and Jimmy take Angela on this trip. It would be a nice way for us to get to know each other as well, and give you a little time to yourself. I think you need to treat yourself to a day of relaxation."

"I would love that!" Angela said, and looked at her mother with wide eyes. "Can I? Can I go on the boat trip and see the alligators, Mom?"

Shannon exhaled and looked into her daughter's eyes begging for a yes. How she loved her dearly and wanted to see her happy. Besides, her sister was right. It would be great to have a day alone to try and figure out her life. She really needed that. She needed peace and quiet to think.

"Can I, Mom? Please? Pretty please?"

It was funny how her daughter always seemed to think the appearance of the word please was important, but it worked, almost every time.

"Okay, then. But you behave, young lady. You do every-thing your Aunt Kristi tells you to, all right?"

Angela saluted like a soldier. "Yes, Ma'am."

Shannon smiled and kissed her sister on the cheek. "See you tomorrow then."

"We'll pick her up around nine tomorrow morning. How does that sound?" Kristi asked.

"Perfect," Shannon said, and grabbed Angela's hand. She looked exhausted. It had been a long and eventful day for her daughter. She took her in her arms and carried her to the car, then shut the door. Kristi and Jimmy came outside.

"So, does anyone know you're here?" Kristi asked.

"So far, I've managed to keep it a secret. I hope to continue to keep it that way."

"That's good," Kristi said with a worried face. "We don't

want this bastard to find you." She touched Shannon's bruised cheek gently with her finger. "You sure you don't want to stay with us, though? We have room for the both of you."

Shannon shook her head. "No, I'm fine at the motel. They're very nice people. I don't want to impose on you guys. Who knows? We might stay for a long time." Shannon stopped. She thought about the officer that had pulled her over and whether he would be able to keep quiet. He had to. He simply had to. Shannon decided to not tell her sister about it; she would only worry.

"Well, I'd better get going before Angela falls asleep. See you tomorrow."

"Be careful," Kristi said, still with deep worried eyes that Shannon remembered from their childhood, growing up with a drunk mother with a failed career as a singer.

61

February 2015

I was quiet in the car all the way to Melbourne Beach. I was worn out after a stressful morning of trying to get the twins ready on time. They had been arguing all morning, and it was a nightmare just to get them to get dressed. On top of it, we had overslept, so they missed the bus, and I had to drive them to school myself. Weasel, who had wanted to come with me to talk to the parents of Janelle Jackson, was very focused and pensive as we drove down A1A. We hit the city sign and turned right into a gated community. We showed our badges to the guard and told him they were expecting us.

"Strange to have a breaking and entering in a gated community, don't you think?" I asked, as we were let through.

"It happens," she said.

I had told her my theory at the office as soon as I had come in that morning, but she hadn't quite bought into it yet. She still believed the judge was the target for the fire, and that we should focus on his murder instead of Melanie Schultz's. But, she agreed to look into the angle of the cheating woman, and I arranged for us to meet with Janelle's parents at their house.

"Finally, someone is listening to us," the mother said, as soon as we had sat down in their kitchen. The house was impeccable, so clean I found no dust anywhere, and all surfaces had been wiped down recently. The house smelled of bleach.

Mrs. Jackson looked at her husband, who was sitting next to her holding her hand. They had that air of sadness about them. Their eyes met briefly. I hated to drag them through this, having to tell their story again, but I sensed they wanted to. They wanted us to take up the case again.

"We never believed it was a breaking and entering," Mr. Jackson said.

Mrs. Jackson shook her head. She was small and dark-haired. She looked so fragile, so delicate, like fine china that could break any moment now.

"The reason why we've come today is we believe there might be a connection to a recent murder committed in Cocoa Beach," I said.

"Cocoa Beach?" Mrs. Jackson said.

"Yes. There seem to be similarities with our case and your daughter's, and we want to know if there are others we can use in our investigation. We can't promise you that our investigation will lead to anything, but we'll do everything we can."

Mrs. Jackson nodded again. "Thank you," she said.

"So, tell us what happened," Weasel said.

They looked at each other again, like they were deciding who should do the talking. Mrs. Jackson started out.

"It was in April of 2002. The seventh of April. We had been invited to our friends' house; actually, they were our neighbors back then. Right across the street from us. We asked Janelle if she wanted to come with us, but she said she didn't feel like it. You know how teenagers are. Everything their parents do is lame. So, we let her stay home. The police later explained to us that she was on the computer most of the night, playing Sims. It was her favorite game."

Mrs. Jackson paused at the painful memory.

"The case file also states that she spoke with someone on the phone," I said. I had been reading the file all morning, trying desperately to find something that I could use.

"She called her boyfriend at the time," Mr. Jackson said. "His name was Alex. He was supposed to come over, but his parents had grounded him because he had been caught on the beach drinking beer. He was interrogated by the police, but there was no evidence to lead to his arrest."

"Anyway," Mrs. Jackson continued. "We got back around eleven-thirty and..." she stopped. The words seemed like they were stuck in her throat.

"We found her in the bathroom," Mr. Jackson said. There was a light tremor to his voice as he continued. "Naked...her eyes staring into the ceiling. She was so pale. I knew right away she was dead, still I tried...you know, you've gotta try...can't give up hope."

"So you performed CPR?" I asked.

Mrs. Jackson put a hand on her husband's shoulder. Tears were streaming across her cheeks now.

"You have to try, don't you? I didn't want to accept it...I couldn't..."

The old memories were unpleasant for the couple, and we let them take their time to get through the pain.

"I'm a little interested in Janelle's love life," I said, after a short while of silence. "I know it's not easy for you to talk about. And forgive me for the character of my question, but do you know if Janelle ever cheated on her boyfriend?"

The couple looked at one another, then back at me. "Yes, as a matter of fact she did. She cheated on her old boyfriend, the one before Alex. It was a year before she died. At a dance at the school, she kissed Alex when she was still going out with someone else," Mrs. Jackson said. "How did you know?"

Weasel and I exchanged looks. Finally, something was adding up in this case.

"Where is Alex today?" I asked. "Do you know where we can find him?"

"You can't. He...He was killed in a car accident four months later," Mr. Jackson said.

62

February 2015

K risti loved spending the day with her niece. Her husband Jimmy seemed to enjoy it just as much, if not more. It was bittersweet for Kristi to watch that sparkle in Jimmy's eyes when he spoke to Angela. To know that she could never give him what he always wanted most in this world, even though he never said so in front of Kristi.

"Can I get an ice cream?" Angela asked, as they passed a small shop on their way to the airboat.

"Not now," Kristi said. "We can't take it on the boat. When we're done, we can all get one. How does that sound?"

"Yay," Angela said. "I want chocolate."

She was such a pretty girl. She looked so much like her mother when she was that age. Kristi remembered her well. She had always loved her youngest sister the most, even though she always got them in trouble. She was the black sheep of the family, but sometimes the black sheep was also the one that was most loved. Shannon still had that ability. She could get herself into deep trouble and still be the most loved person in the world. Everybody adored her. The great country singer, the world-famous celebrity. Kristi couldn't help being a little jealous of her sister every now and then. Especially when she read about her in the magazines in line at the grocery store. They always made her life seem so glamorous. So out of reach for ordinary people like Kristi. Back when it happened, she hadn't known why Shannon suddenly cut her off. At times, she had thought her sister simply had become too big a name to be around her very ordinary sister. Being idolized by the entire world had to do something to you, didn't it? At least that's what Kristi had thought. But, when her sister suddenly showed up in her town telling her story, Kristi had felt ashamed of how she had been thinking about her. Shannon was nothing like she imagined, like she had read about in the magazines. She was still the same good old Shannon that Kristi loved dearly. She was still her baby sister.

"I'll go buy the tickets," Jimmy said, and left them.

Kristi felt Angela's hand in hers and looked down. "I wish I had a sister," Angela said. "I bet you and my mom had fun when you were kids."

Kristi chuckled. "We did. We were quite the troublemakers, the two of us."

"There were three girls, right?"

"Yes. There's also Liz. She was the middle child. She lives in New York."

"How come I haven't been here to visit you before?" Angela asked.

Kristi exhaled. She spotted Jimmy with the tickets coming out of the shop. She smiled. "I don't know, sweetie. You live very far away."

"I wish I could live here," she said. "It's much more fun here."

"Well, you can come visit anytime you want to. Will that do?" Kristi asked, as Jimmy caught up with them and they got in line for the boat.

"I'd like that," Angela said and walked aboard.

They got earplugs to protect their ears from the noise of the boat, and soon they took off. Their guide was a guy in his thirties wearing a bandana. He found several alligators in the swamps and navigated the boat as close as possible, so they could all take pictures. It was a gorgeous trip, Kristi thought, and Angela was beyond excited.

This is what it feels like to be a real family.

They had thought about adopting, but never really gotten around to it. Kristi wasn't sure she wanted to do it. She didn't want some troubled kid. Who knows what a kid like that had been through?

They had never done anything but talk about adopting, and now it was getting too late for them. She was pushing forty and Jimmy forty-five. Did she regret it? Right now, she did. When holding Angela's hand in hers and looking at the animals from the boat, she regretted it bitterly.

An hour later, they were back on land.

"What a great trip," Jimmy said. "I'm so glad I took the day off for this."

"Me too," Kristi said.

"I need to pee," Angela said.

"There's a restroom right over there," Jimmy said, and pointed at the red building.

"I'll take you," Kristi said, and walked with Angela's hand in hers towards the building. "I'll wait out here," she said, and let Angela go inside.

Jimmy signaled that he would get ice cream for all of them. When he returned, Angela still hadn't come out.

"You think she's all right in there?" he asked.

"I hope so. I'll go in and check."

Kristi opened the door and went inside. There were three stalls. "Angela?" she asked. "Are you all right?"

There was no answer. Kristi's heart stopped. All of the doors were open. A back door to the building was ajar.

Oh, my God. She's not here!

63

February 2015

"**A**NGELA IS MISSING!**"**

Shannon was almost screaming on the other end of the line. I looked at Weasel across my desk. There were papers everywhere. We had all the old boxes sent over from the case of Janelle Jackson, and we were going through every little detail.

Weasel caught my alarmed look.

"They don't know where she is. Oh, Jack. You were the only one I could think of to call. Can you help me?"

"Calm down, Shannon. What happened?" I asked.

"My sister Kristi took Angela on an airboat ride. When they were done, she went to the restroom up there, and now they just called and told me they can't find her. They've searched the entire area, but she's not there. Oh, God, Jack. What if Joe has her? What will I do?"

"Where are you now?"

"I'm on my way to Lone Cabbage."

"I'll meet you up there."

I hung up and looked at Weasel.

"What's going on?" she asked.

"Missing child," I said. "By the airboats in Lone Cabbage. I have to get up there."

Weasel smiled. "Well, what are you waiting for? She obviously means a lot to you. I think we're done here for now anyway."

I rushed to my car and drove towards Lone Cabbage. It was located around thirty miles from Cocoa Beach on the mainland where the river mouthed into a big lake. It took me less than twenty minutes to get there with blaring sirens. I arrived almost at the same time as Shannon.

"Jack. I'm so glad you came," she said, approaching me. "I don't know what to do. This is my sister, Kristi, and her husband, Jimmy." I shook hands with all of them. Anxious eyes followed me as they showed Shannon and me to the restrooms where Angela had disappeared.

"She went in through the door and I waited for her out here. I didn't know there was a back door," Kristi said.

A local officer had been called to the scene. I greeted him and told him who I was. We were still in Brevard County, so I was still within my jurisdiction.

"We walked through the area by the boats, and they even sailed out on the water to look for her. We've been everywhere," Jimmy said.

I looked around. There was a lot of dense forest surrounding the area. If she had run in there, it would be very difficult to find her. I remembered a year ago when a child got lost in woods like these and wasn't found until three days later. It was a terrifying time for everyone. The animals living in there weren't joking around.

"Is there any reason to believe she ran away?" I asked. "How was she before she went inside the restroom?"

Kristi shook her head. The shock on her face was visible. She couldn't grasp how this could have happened. "She was good. She seemed happy. We were about to have ice cream. I...I don't see why..."

"He has her," Shannon said with a trembling voice. "I know he does. This has Joe written all over it."

"I thought he didn't know you were here?" I asked.

She shook her head and bit her lip. "He must have found

out somehow. He does stuff like that. He knows people everywhere."

"Have you tried to call him?" I asked.

"Constantly. But he's not picking up," Shannon said. "I'll try again." She pressed her phone frantically. I could tell she was having a hard time holding it together. She had told me about her former drug abuse before she had Angela. I wondered if she craved a drink or a fix right now. I wished I could do more for her.

"Hello? Joe?"

I froze and looked at her. Her eyes sparkled with hope and desperation. "Joe? Joe? You bastard. Where is Angela?"

64

February 2015

"He says he doesn't have her. Where is she, Jack?"

Shannon looked at me like she expected me to have an answer.

"I don't know. I'll start a search," I said. "I'll call in the Sheriff's Department and we'll look for her all night long if we have to. Don't worry."

Shannon put her head on my shoulder. I stroked her hair gently. Suddenly, I missed my kids like crazy.

"I still think he has her," Shannon said. "I think he's lying. It makes sense. Why would he tell me he has her? I would only demand to get her back."

"I guess you're right. But, he's all the way back in Nashville, isn't he?"

"He didn't say. He hung up before I could ask." Shannon sighed. "I have a feeling he's around here somewhere."

I didn't want to say it out loud, but if he had Angela, he would probably be on the road by now…trying to get as far away from here as possible.

"I'll make a few calls," I said. "I'll get the search started, have the dogs come out."

I called Ron, and an hour later, all of my colleagues from the Sheriff's Department arrived and started the search. There were dogs, helicopters, and lots of volunteers, who helped walk through the forest in search of Angela. I felt grateful for every one of them. So did Shannon.

But as nightfall came, they still hadn't found her. Shannon was on the verge of breaking down, and I decided to take her back to the motel.

"But I want to stay here. In case she shows up," she said.

"There are hundreds of people here," I said. "If they find her, I promise you'll be the first to know. You need to get some rest. I'm taking you back now."

Shannon finally agreed to let me drive her back. She was sobbing and crying most of the way. I wanted to comfort her, but it was just so difficult. I was afraid of saying the wrong thing.

"We'll find her. Don't worry," I said for the tenth time, when I drove up in front of the motel. I had asked my mother to take care of the kids, and they were all asleep in their extra bedroom when we arrived. I let them stay in there and closed the door, kissed my mother thank you, then helped Shannon get to her room. I opened the door, and with her leaning on me, I helped her get to the bed. She took one glance at Angela's empty bed and her stuffed animals on top of it, then burst into tears.

"Oh, my baby. Where is she, Jack? Where is she?"

I let her cry in my arms, while I stroked her hair gently. Even when crying she was beautiful. Her hands touched my face and she pulled me closer.

"You need to get some sleep," I said. "Lay down. I'll stay with you till you fall asleep."

"I can't," she said. "I can't sleep without my daughter."

"Listen to me," I said. "You think Joe has her, right?"

She sniffled. "Yes. Yes I do."

"Would he ever hurt Angela?"

She looked pensive for a second, then shook her head. "No, not Angela. Me, he would, but Angela is his diamond. He loves her more than he loves himself."

"So, if we assume she's with Joe, then we must assume she's fine, right? He'll take proper care of her, right?"

Shannon scoffed. A hint of a smile spread across her face. "You make a very good point, Detective Jack Ryder."

"Now, get some sleep. Tomorrow, we'll look for Joe, and then we'll get Angela back to you."

Shannon put her head on the pillow and closed her eyes. "You're a very sweet man, Jack Ryder," she mumbled. "You're very good at saying the right things."

I leaned over and kissed her cheek, like I kissed my children's when tucking them in. It made her smile.

65

February 2015

S hannon woke up with a start.

"Angela?" she cried wearily. "Angela?"

She had dreamt about her daughter. She had dreamt that she had held her in her arms again. Now, there was nothing but the darkness…the vast gloom of the night. Realizing that her daughter was still missing, that it was nothing but a dream, Shannon sobbed. She pulled her legs up underneath her chin and cried. She tried to close her eyes and go back to sleep, but had no success. She turned around and spotted Jack. He was sitting in the chair, his head resting on the wall behind him, his mouth open. His eyes were closed, and he was snoring lightly.

"You're going to wake up with a pain in your neck," she whispered, but couldn't help smiling. Jack was usually so handsome, but right now, he didn't look very attractive. He was drooling slightly.

Shannon tilted her head and looked at him. She couldn't believe he had stayed here for her sake. They had only known each other for a short while, yet she felt so incredibly attracted to him, like they had known each other always.

She stared at him for a long time, wondering if he had planned on staying here, or if he had simply fallen asleep while waiting.

Either way, it was nice to have him here. He made her feel secure, like nothing bad could ever reach her. He had a way of making people feel comfortable when they were around him. It was a very rare quality in a man.

"Who are you, Jack Ryder?" she whispered in the darkness. Outside, the full moon was making it a very bright night. Shannon sat up in the bed, wondering how Angela was doing, if she was all right, if she was scared or even crying? She kind of hoped Joe had her, since she knew she would at least be safe. But, then again. Would she ever see her again? Would Joe let her? Would they have to go through a custody battle? The drug abuse would come up. Shannon traveled all the time. That would be an issue as well. She had no proof that Joe had hit her, she never reported it, and never took pictures of the abuse. They would have to rely on witnesses, and when it came to having friends who would testify on your behalf, Joe by far surpassed her. She had no friends of her own. They were all Joe's.

"Damn you, Joe," she whispered.

Jack grumbled something in his sleep, then moved his head. It fell down, and he started nodding. Shannon chuckled. She longed to feel the warmth of another body close to hers. She longed to have warm arms around her making her feel like she was safe. Shannon cried silently, thinking about all the nights Joe had yelled at her for hours…yelled and slapped her around. The past fifteen years with him had been a living hell. How had she not had the strength to leave him before?

Because she was afraid of him. She was terrified that he would do something like what he had done today. She was so afraid she would never see her daughter again. And now, it had happened. He had taken her, and for all she knew, he could be on his way to Mexico with her in the car.

Shannon sobbed at the thought. She loathed how she had felt angst every day of her life. Anxious about what he would come up with next, what would set him off. The man she was supposed to feel secure with, the one person in the world that was supposed to protect her, had been the source of all her misery. It was all so clear now. But it wasn't over, just because she had decided to leave him. That was very clear to her now. Was it ever going to be over?

Shannon couldn't stop the tears. She tried to wipe them away, but more came as fast as she removed them. Suddenly, she felt someone come up behind her. Warmth spread over her entire body as he leaned in and kissed her on the neck.

"Jack," she whispered. He put his arm around her and pulled her close to him, while kissing her neck and throat. Shannon moaned and leaned her head back. His touches made her tears stop. She whispered his name again, right before she closed her eyes and let herself get into the moment.

66

February 2015

I woke up in Shannon's arms. It was still early morning. I managed to get myself out of her embrace, then kissed her on the cheek before I reached for my pants and my phone. It was still only a quarter to six. I had fifteen minutes before the kids had to get up and get ready for school.

I looked at the sleeping Shannon. I couldn't believe myself. I never did anything like this. I had taken a chance. I had woken up and found her crying. I couldn't believe I had dared to simply kiss her, but I had wanted to so badly. I wanted to be close to her. She was in such deep pain, and I wanted to simply comfort her, but one thing led to another.

Shannon groaned in her sleep. She looked more beautiful than ever. I felt a pinch of joy in my heart. I really liked her, and I hoped I hadn't ruined everything by sleeping with her. It was beautiful…what we shared. It was so intimate, and even though I did feel guilty, since I was technically still married, and so was she, I couldn't help feeling happy.

I picked up my shirt and got dressed, then leaned over and whispered in her ear. "I need to go, Shannon. The kids are waiting for me. I'll be back once I've put them on the bus, all right?"

Shannon opened her eyes. She smiled. She grabbed my

collar and pulled me closer, then kissed me. The kiss was soft and gentle. Kissing her stirred things up inside of me in a way it never had with any other girl. Not even with Arianna.

I just hoped she felt the same way.

"I'll be back," I whispered.

"Okay," she moaned, then went back to sleep. I was glad she finally managed to get some rest. She needed it.

I put on my shoes, then went outside and closed the door carefully, to not wake up Shannon once again, then ran for my condo, where I found new clothes for myself and for the children. I took a very quick shower, then hurried to my parent's quarters at the motel. The kids were still heavily asleep when I entered the bedroom my parents had made for them. Even Emily had crashed there on the futon.

"Guys. It's time to get up," I whispered.

"Dad," Abigail moaned, while slowly coming to life. I leaned in and kissed her. She grabbed me by the neck and hugged me. It felt good. I thought about Shannon. I couldn't imagine not knowing where my kids were. It was unbearable.

"Did you find Angela?" Austin asked. He was sitting up in his bed above Abigail's. I stood up and looked at him. He looked so cute in his little PJs with airplanes on them. Part of me hoped he would never grow out of this stage.

"No, buddy. Not yet. But, we'll find her. We believe she is with her dad."

"Then why don't you just call him and ask?" Abigail asked.

"We did," I said, and threw their clothes on their beds so they could get dressed. Emily went to the bathroom and took a shower. She was always grumpy in the mornings, and I always let her take her time to wake up.

"So, what's the problem, then?" Abigail asked.

"Well, honey, it's not that easy. See, her father says he doesn't have her, but he might not be telling the truth."

"Why wouldn't he tell the truth?" Abigail asked.

I shrugged. "I don't know. Maybe because he doesn't want us to find her."

"That's stupid," Abigail said, and started putting on her clothes. I could hear my mother in the kitchen. I was starving.

"Grown-ups do a lot of stupid things," I said. "Now, get ready. I don't want you to miss the bus again."

February 2015

S hannon had no idea what to do. She took a shower, while wondering if she had made a mistake. It was way too early for her to get involved with someone else, wasn't it? But how could it be wrong if it felt so good? If it felt so right?

The old bathtub was clogged, and soon her feet were in ankle-deep water. She put shampoo in her hair and rubbed it thoroughly, then rinsed, and soon the water in the tub was up to her shins. She turned off the water for a little while to let it run down the drain. It went slowly. As soon as it reached her ankles again, she turned the shower back on and put conditioner in her hair. She shaved her legs while the conditioner sunk in, then rinsed it all out. She closed her eyes and thought about last night with Jack and how wonderful he had made her feel.

What is this? She thought to herself. Did she want to be with him again? Yes. She desperately wanted to feel him close to her again. But, was it right? Was it too early for her? Joe would kill her if he found out. And he'd kill Jack as well. She was terrified of dragging Jack into her complicated life, into something he couldn't get himself out of.

It was all a mess.

Shannon let the water wash over her face, thinking about

Angela and how she was the only thing that mattered now. The rest had to wait.

"I miss you, baby girl. Where are you?" she whispered, when turning off the shower. The water was now to her knees.

The plumbing at this motel is awful, she thought to herself, and walked out of the tub, expecting the water to drain. It did a little while she got dressed, but as she turned on the faucet to brush her teeth, something happened. Instead of water running down the drain, water spurted out of it and hit Shannon in the face. The water smelled terrible, like it was rotten, and Shannon shrieked. She looked at her face in the mirror.

What is this?

Shannon looked down at the sink, where murky water was rising from the drain. She turned and looked at the bathtub, where the water had suddenly sucked out, and now it was spurting what looked like muddy water back out of it.

Shannon clasped her face, then ran out of the bathroom while yelling.

"Jaaack!"

She opened the door and ran out to the parking lot. Jack was standing by the road with his kids waiting for the bus. He turned to look at her when he heard his name. The bus came at the same instant, and he helped the kids get inside, then he hurried towards her.

"What's going on?" he asked, terrified. "What's that on you?"

"I...I don't know. It just came out of the drain, it spurted right into my face. It smells disgusting."

"I think we need to call for a plumber. I'm on it. Do you have some other clothes? You can shower at my place. It's a newer condominium; we have better plumbing. My parents constantly have problems down here."

Shannon went back to her room and found a dress she could change into. She felt nauseated by the smell in the room and on her. She hurried out of there and followed Jack to his condo. They met his parents on the way.

"The plumbing is acting up again, Dad," Jack said. "Tell the other guests to not use the showers or flush the toilets until it's fixed."

Jack showed Shannon into his condo, which turned out to be a pleasant surprise. Shannon had expected it to be a real bachelor pad, but it was nicely decorated and, of course, filled with children's toys everywhere and drawings they had made and that he had put on the walls. It was big too. Four bedrooms.

Shannon hurried into the shower, while Jack called the local plumber. She scrubbed herself thoroughly to get the smell away. When she was done, she still felt like it was in her hair, and on her body. What was it? Sewer mud? It smelled so rotten. The mere thought of it made her want to throw up.

Shannon put on her dress, and then returned to Jack in the living room. The condo was located on the third floor and had spectacular views of the Atlantic from every window. Jack hung up the phone just as she walked in.

"The sewer is probably just clogged up again," he said. "The guy will fix it. Now we need to focus on finding Angela. I just got off the phone with one of my colleagues at the station. He tells me Joe has been seen in one of the resorts downtown. He checked in two days ago."

68

February 2015

"**W**HERE IS SHE?"
Shannon stared at Joe. He was standing in the door to his room at the International Resort. I stayed a few feet behind her, making sure he knew I was there, in case he tried anything. I made my weapon in my belt visible, to make sure he knew he couldn't do anything.

Joe stared back at Shannon. "You mean to say you haven't found her yet?" he asked. His voice was agitated as he spoke.

"Don't give me that," Shannon said, and pushed him aside. She went inside the room. Joe stepped back and let me walk in as well.

"Angela?" Shannon called. "Angela, sweetie?"

There was no answer. Joe was sizing me up. It made me feel uncomfortable. He was a big guy. Bigger than me.

"Shannon, Goddammit," Joe said. "I told you I don't have her! Do you mean to tell me you don't know where she is?"

I was starting to get an alarming feeling in my body. Something was very wrong here. Joe's voice cracked when he spoke. He was clearly upset about this.

"I thought you found her," Joe said. "Since you didn't call me back last night, I thought she had come back. You mean to tell me our daughter has been missing since yesterday?"

"Why would I call you back, Joe? You hung up on me," Shannon said.

"I hung up because I got so pissed at you. I thought it was some gimmick on your part to pretend like she had gone missing, maybe because you wanted to hide her from me. I don't know."

"Now, why would I do that, Joe?" Shannon asked.

"I don't know. But since I didn't hear from you again, I thought it wasn't important. I figured that if she really had run away from you, she had come back. I expected you to at least let me know."

Shannon approached Joe, her jaws clenched. "You're lying," she said. "You have her somewhere. Where is she, Joe? Tell me!"

"I don't know," he said.

The scene was getting absurd. I was starting to believe him.

"Yes, you do," Shannon continued relentlessly. "You've hidden her somewhere, haven't you? Taken her somewhere else to make sure I never find her again."

"I can't say the thought hasn't crossed my mind more than once," he said. "But, unfortunately, that is not the case. I haven't seen her since you took her away and left without a word."

They stood in front of each other like cocks before a fight. Shannon was growling in anger. Joe had his fist clenched. I was beginning to fear this was going to end badly.

"Shannon," I said. "She's clearly not here. Let's go."

Shannon lifted a finger and pointed at Joe. "This isn't over yet."

"I sure hope not," Joe said. "She's my daughter too. I want to find her as badly as you do."

Shannon growled, then walked past me. I looked at Joe, then gave him my card and told him not to leave town.

"I don't intend to," he said. "Not without my daughter."

I followed Shannon into the hallway. She was grumbling

and mumbling and hitting her fist into the walls as we approached the elevator.

"Can you believe that guy?" she asked, when we were in the elevator and I had pushed the button.

"What if he's telling the truth?" I asked. "What if he doesn't have her?"

The realization made my stomach turn. If Joe didn't have Angela, then who the hell did? Had she, after all, run into the forest…maybe to get away from her aunt and uncle? Maybe because she was going through a rough time with her mom and dad splitting up and all? I had spoken to the search team earlier on the phone, and they had searched the forest around the lake all night and found nothing, no trace of Angela, not even a footprint or a piece of clothing. The dogs hadn't even picked up her smell beyond the area surrounding the restroom. It was all very odd.

"He has her," Shannon said. "I know he does."

Maybe it was for the best that Shannon insisted on believing that. At least it was a lot better than the scenarios that were playing out in my head.

69

February 2015

He had done something stupid. Was this going to be the mistake that would put him in jail? The Snakecharmer wondered, while staring at the girl on the bed. He had sedated her. He had stuck a cloth with chloroform in her face and held it there till she passed out. That way he had been able to get her out of the restroom without anyone noticing. He had carried her over his shoulder, pretending like she was asleep and he was her father. No one wondered. It was the easiest thing in the world.

Now, he had three children to take care of.

"Are you running a day-care now?" the Snakecharmer's father said from his wheelchair in the corner of the living room. Angela had just woken up and had started screaming so loudly he had to gag her. Now, she was squirming on the bed, trying to get out of the duct tape he had bound her hands and feet with.

"What are you going to do with all these kids?" his dad asked.

The Snakecharmer didn't answer...for the simple reason that he had no idea. It had seemed like such a great idea when he had first thought about it, a perfect way to punish Shannon King for cheating on her husband, but the Snakecharmer hadn't thought it through properly.

"I had to help her," he said.

"She was in trouble?" the dad asked.

"Yes," he said, thinking about how glad she should be that he had taken her away from all the trouble that was about to erupt in her life. She had no idea...of course she didn't. Children never knew how much it was going to affect them that their parents messed around. This world was filled with parents, especially women, who thought they could just fool around and never think about how much it affected someone else's life. How it destroyed everything for a family.

"It's always the children that get hurt," he said.

"True," his father said.

Earlier in the day, he had been at the motel, dressed in a female fat-suit, a dress and wig, like he always was when going there, but the place had been crawling with police cars, and he had no chance of getting in. He knew then that they would soon be on to him. It was about time he got the hell out of here.

The Snakecharmer found the cloth with chloroform and wet it again, before he placed it over the mouth of the girl. He had packed a couple of suitcases that he placed in the back of the truck while Angela dozed off. He put Will in the back seat and asked the boy to sit next to him, in case he needed anything. He packed his dad's car and put the sleeping Angela in the back seat with the other children. He had colored her hair while she was out and cut it short, so no one would be able to recognize her. These children were going with him, and he was going to take proper care of them. He wasn't going to let them down like their parents had. There was only one thing wrong with this plan.

He couldn't bring his father.

His dad was way too old and sick to travel this far by car. He would only be confused, since he couldn't see anything, and when they moved around, it would be too much for him. The Snakecharmer hadn't told him they were leaving; he simply didn't have the heart to do so. So now, he knelt in front of him and put his father's hand on his head.

"What's wrong, Son?" his dad asked and felt his face.

He wanted to say he was sorry for everything. Sorry for what had happened to him, sorry for bringing him trouble, sorry for leaving him, sorry for stealing his car without asking, but he didn't. He couldn't. Instead, he simply smiled and said, "I'm just going to Publix. I'll take the kids. Give you some quiet time. Do you want me to bring you anything?"

His father smiled. Then he nodded. "Oh, you sweet kid. Yes. Bring me some…"

"Cake and beer," the Snakecharmer said, when a tear escaped the corner of his eye. He sniffled and got up. "I'll bring you cake and beer when I come back."

"Thank you, Son. You're a good boy."

70

February 2015

I couldn't believe it. When we got back to the motel, it was blocked by police cars. Even the ME was there. Weasel was in the parking lot talking to my parents. My colleagues were questioning the guests.

"What the heck is going on?" Shannon asked.

"I have no idea."

I stepped out of the car. Weasel approached me when she saw me. "Jack. Where the hell have you been? I've been calling you like crazy."

I reached into my pocket and pulled out my phone. "The sound's been shut off. I'm sorry. What's going on here?"

"What's going on? I'll tell you what. Hell on earth…that's what." Weasel sighed and rubbed the bridge of her nose. "You called the plumber this morning, right? You called Eric, right?"

"Yes. The sewer was clogged," I said.

"I bet it was," Weasel said. "Eric went in, and you'll never guess what he found." She paused for effect. "That's right. First, he found the drain to be packed with a flesh-like substance. Then he called his supervisor to assess the situation, thinking it looked like chicken meat, maybe from the restaurant. By the time they cleared the drain, they realized, on closer inspection, that it wasn't chicken leftovers. It was small bones and flesh. The pipe leading off from the drain was completely clogged with it. Yamilla is looking at it as we speak, but her first suspicion was that it was of human origin."

I felt sick to my stomach. I looked at Shannon, who was paler than Weasel's white shirt.

"Someone tried to dispose of a body," Weasel continued. "By chopping it up, then flushing it."

"Oh, my God," I said.

"I know," Weasel said. "We are going to have to shut down the motel and your parents and their guests will have to find somewhere else to stay. I will also need your parents to stay in town."

"They didn't do it," I said angrily.

"I know they're probably innocent," Weasel said. "But until I can determine that for certain, they are our main suspects. I'm sorry, Jack. That's just the way it is. You know how these things work."

I did, and that was what scared the crap out of me. My parents had nothing to do with this. I knew they didn't, but I had to find evidence to prove it; otherwise, they would end up paying the price for this.

My mom looked terrified while she was speaking to Sheriff Ron. My dad had put his arm around her shoulder. I approached them.

"We have no idea. You must believe us," my mom said. When she saw me, her face lit up. I hugged her. She was shivering. Ron saw me and nodded.

"I was done here, anyway," he said and put a hand on my shoulder. "We'll figure this out. Don't worry."

"Thanks, Ron."

"Oh, Jack. This is terrible. What do we do?" my mother said. It was terrible to see her in this much distress. My dad looked pale and tired. This was too much commotion for him. For the both of them. I had to get them out of here.

I reached into my pocket and found the keys to my condo. I was so angry my hands were trembling.

"You stay at my place till this blows over. Now, tell me, where do I find a list of all your guests over the last three months?"

"The guestbook in the lobby," my mother said, her voice trembling. "But surely…you can't think that any of our guests could have…"

"Oh, I'm certain they did," I said. "And I'm going to find out who it was and bring them to justice. You trust in that. It just got personal."

Part Three

HIT THE ROAD

71

February 2015

T wo days later, we had a clearer picture of what had happened at my parents' motel. I had worked the crime scene with Yamilla for hours and hours and had very little sleep. The kids stayed with their grandparents at my condo, and so did Shannon. It had become a little cramped, but it worked out. Shannon wanted to check into a hotel, but I told her it was a bad idea for her to be alone. I think she agreed. She didn't protest.

So now, we were all living under the same roof. Luckily, my condo was big enough, even though it meant the three kids all had to sleep in the same room, not that they complained about that. On the contrary, they thought it was a party. Well, the twins did. Emily…not so much. But she didn't complain. My parents made sure the children were taken care of and made it to school while I worked.

By the end of the second day, Weasel came down to the motel and we went through what we knew so far.

"There seem to be two bodies," Yamilla said. "We're running the DNA samples to try to compare them with those of Melanie and Sebastian Schultz. They are the two missing persons we have around here, and therefore, the two most likely to be a match."

I took over. "Meanwhile, we have located the room where

the body parts were being flushed from. Room one-fifteen. It's the room where Shannon King stayed with her daughter when the sewer clogged, but she hasn't been in it for very long. We believe it was the guest before her, last month, when Melanie and her son disappeared who did this, then vanished afterwards."

"Well, do we have a name?" Weasel asked.

"According to the books my parents kept, it was a Mrs. Hampton who stayed there for the whole month of January."

"A woman?" Weasel said. "What do we know about her?"

"She's been a regular for almost a year. Coming and going. Sometimes, she stays for several weeks at a time. She checked in on January 3rd this year and stayed till January 29th, then came back a week ago on February 23rd and stayed in another room. She hasn't checked out, hasn't paid for her stay this time, but her room is empty."

"Any fingerprints?"

"The room hasn't been cleaned yet, so I'm hoping. So far, they haven't found anything. The techs just started working her room this morning. According to Jennifer, the cleaning lady at the motel, Mrs. Hampton never wanted her room cleaned while she was there, which is always respected. Jennifer remembers when Mrs. Hampton checked out in January from room one-fifteen. It was so clean, she hardly had to clean it. She believed Mrs. Hampton had cleaned it herself. Everything smelled like bleach, she said."

"Bleach, you say?" Weasel said and looked at me.

"I know. It sounds awfully familiar, doesn't it?" I said.

"What else do we know about this Mrs. Hampton?" Weasel asked.

"Not much," I said. "I've seen her around here. I remember helping her with her suitcase last time she checked in. She told my parents she lives up north, outside of Boston, and she comes here as often as she can to get away from the cold. I've tried to locate her, but she hasn't made it easy. Always paid cash. She left no trace. I don't even know which town outside of Boston she is from."

"So, she could basically vanish if she wanted to. I don't like this, Ryder. I really don't." Weasel exhaled.

I looked at Yamilla. "It's all we've got so far," I said. She confirmed it with a nod.

"So, what we believe now is that this woman brought bodies to the motel and dismembered them. She then flushed the body parts into the toilet?" Weasel sighed. "I...Is it really possible?"

"It's been done before," Yamilla said. "Dennis Nilsen was a killer in London who lured men into his apartment, then killed them and dismembered their bodies before he flushed them into the toilet. A lot like what happened here."

"Jeffrey Dahmer did something similar," I said.

"Yes, but he dissolved the body parts in acid first. He was smarter," Yamilla said. "He didn't clog the sewer."

"He also crushed the bones with a sledgehammer, but that's not important for this case," I said. "The point is, it has been done before. Our dear Mrs. Hampton might have gotten the idea from reading about Dennis Nilsen. Maybe that would be a trace worth following."

I had barely finished the sentence before my phone rang. It was Shannon. "I gotta take this," I said and stepped aside.

Weasel and Yamilla exchanged looks. They both smiled. "She's got you on speed-dial now?" Weasel said.

I ignored them.

"Jack?"

Her voice sounded upset.

"What's wrong?"

"I...I just got a call. Some guy told me he has Angela. He's asking for money. What do I do, Jack?"

"What? How did he get your number? I thought no one knew it?"

"He called my manager first. Told him he had Angela and that he would kill her if he said anything. Then, he asked for my number. Bruce gave it to him. Said he didn't dare do anything else. Oh, my God, Jack. This guy has my little girl. What do I do?"

72

February 2015

Shannon grabbed a bottle of Xanax from her purse. She looked at herself in the bathroom mirror. Next to her was her phone. Her heart was pounding rapidly in her chest. The guy had sounded so creepy. He had told her he had Angela. She had told him she didn't believe him. Then he had texted her a photo. Angela sitting on a bed. She was still wearing the same dress she had been on the day she had disappeared. Shannon had started crying when she saw it. Angela looked good, though. That had been a comfort. She had a sad look on her face, but she seemed to have been well taken care of. That was a great relief. But after the relief over seeing her alive had settled, unease had rumbled inside of Shannon. The voice on the phone clearly wasn't Joe's. Neither was it one of his friends, none that Shannon knew of at least. It could be someone she had never met, but she was beginning to believe this had nothing to do with Joe anymore. Why would he be asking for money? In a divorce, he would get half of Shannon's money. He would never want for anything.

Angela had been kidnapped by someone else. But, who was he? Was he simply someone who saw an opportunity to score some money? Shannon had been warned about those. When you became a celebrity...that was the price you paid. People would look at you and smell money. Your kids were in constant danger of being abducted for a ransom. Shannon had known about it; she had heard about it and been warned, but never believed it would actually happen to her. Back in Tennessee, they lived a very protected life. Angela went to private school and was never let out of sight. They lived in a gated community with strict security, and they even had security guards of their own patrolling the house to make sure crazy fans didn't somehow come too close. It was the price of being a celebrity.

But, when Shannon had escaped from Joe without leaving a word to anyone else except Bruce, her manager, she had also left that security behind. She had believed she could stay hidden, that she could keep her presence in Cocoa Beach a secret, but now she knew it had been stupid to think so.

You're stupid, Shannon. So incredibly stupid!

Shannon grabbed the bottle of pills and felt it in her hand. She knew it was a bad idea. It was a slippery slope for her to take the pills, but she craved them more than ever. She wanted to make the pain stop, to sedate the voices in her mind that told her she was to blame for this, that it was all her own fault what had happened to Angela. She was going to pay the money. But she needed to calm herself down first.

Shannon opened the top of the bottle and took out a pill. She looked at her face in the mirror, and just as she was about to put it on her tongue, someone knocked on the door.

"Shannon?"

It was Jack. The sound of his voice made her hesitate. She knew very well what would happen to her once she took the pill. She would change. Her personality would alter.

"Shannon? Are you all right?" he said again.

You don't deserve him. He's too good for you.

"I'm fine," she said. "I'll be right out."

She put the pill on her tongue and reached for a glass of water. A strange sound came from behind the door. Someone was tampering with the lock. It clicked, and Jack stood in the doorway.

"Don't do it," he said when he saw the bottle of pills.

"Please don't. You know what will happen. You're an addict. One pill will lead to another, and you won't be able to stop. Please, don't do it. I know it's hard right now. But we'll get your daughter home. At least we know she's alive. At least we have a chance now. Don't ruin it. Don't get her back and then neglect her by being an addict again. It might give you comfort now and make the pain go away for a little while, but it's not worth it, Shannon. Please, think of your daughter."

Shannon stared at the glass of water. The pill was still on her tongue. She felt tears piling up. Jack was right. He was so right. But, could she handle this? Could she go through this without easing the pain? Without sedation?

Shannon looked at herself in the mirror again. The bruises were healing nicely, and soon she would be able to walk around without covering her face. The bruises were connected to that old life of hers. Did she really want to go back to that life? Back to the abuse? The life in a constant daze?

Shannon turned her head towards the toilet, then spat out the pill and flushed. Jack approached her, grabbed her face between his hands and kissed her. She cried and threw herself in his arms. He wiped the tears away from her cheeks, then looked into her eyes.

"Now, let's go get her, shall we?"

"What about your case here? You have a lot on your plate?" Shannon asked. "Your parents…The motel?"

"It will have to wait," Jack said. "Angela is what counts now."

73

February 2015

The kidnapper had told Shannon to meet him at Ponce de Leon Landing, a park with a big parking lot close to Sebastian Inlet. He hadn't told her to come alone, so I insisted on coming along. There was no way she should do this alone. Besides, I was armed and she was not. She needed the protection.

We hit the road together.

Shannon transferred the money to the account she had been told to. It was registered in the Cayman Islands, so there was no way we would be able to trace the money afterwards. Two million dollars gone into cyberspace. Just like that.

With the printed out bank-statement as documentation in our hands, we drove to the parking lot. It was right on the beach, and I could smell the ocean as we got out of Shannon's rented SUV. There was a trail between the trees that led to the beach and the crashing waves. She gave me a terrified look, and I took her by the hand, as we walked to the meeting point, by some statue of Ponce de Leon.

We waited for fifteen minutes and nothing happened. Shannon was getting more and more anxious by the minute, and I couldn't blame her. This was nerve racking. I had never done a ransom exchange before and wondered if I should have gotten Ron and my colleagues at the Sheriff's Department in on it. Just to make sure we caught the bastard. But I had decided not to, and I was sticking to that decision. I didn't want to risk ruining it. Shannon didn't care about the money or the guy. She just wanted Angela back.

"You think he might have seen you and blown us off?" she asked.

"I don't know," I said.

"Oh, my God. We already transferred the money. Do you think he might have just taken it and run away?"

"I'm not going to lie to you, Shannon. It's a possibility. You can't trust a guy like that," I said.

Her eyes lost their light. I didn't like being the one doing that to her, but I had to be realistic. Coming here was dangerous for him. He would be seen. And he had no reason to come. Not now that he had already gotten the money. I told Shannon to tell him she wasn't going to transfer the money until she had Angela, but she didn't dare to. She was afraid of scaring him away and never seeing Angela again. She wanted to do everything he told her to, to make sure nothing went wrong. I couldn't blame her, but it left her with very small odds of actually getting what she wanted.

"You don't think he's coming, do you?" she asked nervously. She was biting her lips constantly. I wanted to take her in my arms and just hold her tight. I hated to see her like this.

Suddenly, something happened. A car drove past on the street. We both looked at it in anticipation, our hearts thumping in our chests. But it wasn't what we expected it to be. It wasn't Angela. Instead, whoever was in the truck, rolled down the window and fired a shot at us.

"Get down," I yelled and jumped on top of Shannon. More shots were fired while we hid behind the statue, before the truck's wheels screeched and it disappeared again.

"Oh, my God. What was that?" Shannon shrieked.

I removed myself from her. "Are you all right?" I asked.

"I think so. Are you?"

"Yes. I wasn't hit either."

"You think that was the kidnapper?" Shannon asked.

"Yes. I believe it must have been."

"But…" Shannon was about to cry. "What about Angela? Where is Angela?"

"She's not here, and I have a feeling she's not going to be either. Come, let's get back to the car. I think I got a look at the license plate. I'm not letting this bastard get away."

74

October 1998

S he was so fed up with her family. Annie served dinner on the night after the incident where her teenage son accidentally caught her on the couch with the handsome officer. She had yelled at him and told him to go to his room, then gone back to the officer, who had told her it was best if he left. She was disappointed to see him go and so angry with her son for interrupting the one good thing she had in her life. Maybe, possibly, destroying it for her. What if seeing her son made the officer have second thoughts? What if he was scared away and decided never to come again?

"Here's the lasagna," she said, and threw the dish on the table.

Victor was smiling from ear to ear, as always when he came home from work. "Smells delicious," he chirped.

What are you so happy about, you ugly pig?

Their son was sitting at the table, looking at her with his small evil eyes, his nostrils flaring. Annie didn't care about him or what he thought he had seen. She was fed up with him, and with Victor as well. She had wasted so much of her life on them.

"So, how was your day, Son?" Victor asked, obviously not noticing the tension between the boy and his mother. That was Victor for you. He never understood what was going on right beneath his nose. He always believed the best in people, with the result that he was always run over by everyone, the wimp.

"Eventful," their son answered, still with his eyes fixated on Annie.

"Wonderful," Victor said, and scooped up the lasagna with his fork. He even ate ugly. Chewed with his mouth open, smacked his lips, and drank noisily. Their dinners were like torture to Annie.

"And you, dear?" Victor said, addressed to Annie.

She sighed. "Nothing much. The usual stuff."

"Wonderful," Victor said.

That was when the boy dropped his fork onto the plate with a loud sound. Annie jumped in her seat.

"That's it!" the boy yelled. "I've had it. Stop pretending everything is fine. Stop acting like we're a happy little family!"

Victor looked, appalled, at his son. "Son, what has gotten into you?"

"I'll tell you what has gotten into me, Dad. Today, I came home early from school, since some of my classes were suspended, and guess who I found? Yes, that's right. Mommy dear on the couch in the arms of another man." He looked at Annie. "That's right. Mom is cheating on you, Dad, and you don't even have a clue."

Victor's face froze. He stared at Annie without making a sound. Annie felt her heart rate go up. Victor scared her a little. She felt bad that he had to find out about it this way. What would he do? How would he react? Would he throw her out? She would have nothing. He wouldn't do that, would he?

"All we ever wanted was for you to love us, Mom," the son continued. "Don't you think I know? Don't you think I've noticed that you've avoided me all my life? Do you really think I don't know that you only tolerate me and Dad in your life?"

Annie swallowed hard. He was right. That was how she

had always felt, but hearing it from his mouth made it sound so awful; it sounded like she was a terrible person.

"Is this true?" Victor asked, his voice trembling. "Did you sleep with someone...here in our home?"

Annie didn't look at him at first. When she did, she saw tears streaming across his cheeks.

"I...Victor...I..."

Victor shook his head. "I can't believe it. I gave you everything. I gave up everything for you. I married you when... when no one else wanted to. I made an honest woman out of you. I bought you that house. I gave up all I had when my mother told me to leave you, when she found out about...that he wasn't my son."

The boy stared at his father, then back at his mother. "Victor is not my real dad?"

It was like the entire ground beneath Annie had opened up and started to swallow her up. She had no idea how to resist falling, how to stay up anymore. There was room for no more lies, no more deceit. She simply couldn't anymore.

"I...I..."

"I can't believe this, Victor said. "You never loved me, did you? You never loved either of us."

Annie had no idea how to answer that, and hesitated just long enough for him to know how she really felt. Victor broke down and cried, then got up and stormed out on the balcony, where he kept all of his chemicals for his pool business. He grabbed a bucket of acid, brought it with him inside, then took one last glance at Annie, and with the words, goodbye, cruel world, he poured the acid over himself.

After that, there was nothing but screaming.

75

February 2015

He felt good about himself. The Snakecharmer felt so good about what he had done. He didn't mean to actually kill them, but he had scared them just enough to let them know he was the one in control. They weren't.

And now, he had the money. He never intended to give the girl back to her awful mother. Not after what she did. Not after she slept with Jack Ryder while still married to someone else. It was simply not tolerated.

Just like he hadn't tolerated it when his own mother had done it. It had destroyed everything for him. His dad had tried to commit suicide, but survived, bound to a wheelchair, blind and disfigured for the rest of his life. And she had done all this to him. She was the one who had destroyed the man.

That was why she had to pay for what she had done. Just like every other woman the Snakecharmer encountered who thought it was okay to mess around while married. But, it wasn't okay; it wasn't something that went by easily. It always destroyed the family, and worst of all, it destroyed the children.

After his dad had come back from the hospital, the Snakecharmer's mother was no longer there. The Snakecharmer told his father she had run away, but it was a lie. The fact was, the Snakecharmer had killed her. She was his first. He had strangled her with his bare hands, then dismembered her and thrown her in a dumpster. No one ever found her. Today, the Snakecharmer knew it had been risky back then, since today he knew better how to dispose of a body. But he had been lucky. Later in life, when his girlfriend had cheated on him, he had killed her too, and made it look like a breaking and entering gone wrong.

He now knew why God had put him on this forsaken planet...he knew what his mission was. He had heard God tell him in church one day. He was to rid the earth of these mothers who ruined everything. He was to save those children who were hurt. That was his mission, and he would live up to it.

For years, he hadn't killed anyone. He married well for himself and didn't find any need to do it, not until the bitch cheated on him. And on top of it, she did it while their daughter had been sleeping in the next room. The Snakecharmer had been away; he had been on one of his casino trips to Atlanta with a friend of his when it happened. His wife had been with her lover when the baby in the next room stopped breathing. She hadn't even noticed until the next morning, when lover boy was gone, and she had finally paid attention to her baby.

Sudden Infant Death Syndrome, they had called it. There wasn't anything she could have done, the doctors told them afterwards. But the Snakecharmer didn't believe that. He believed Laura had killed their baby because she was too busy sleeping with someone else to check on her. Laura believed it too. Till the day he killed her. She knew. She was tormented by guilt. She told him it would never happen again. Yet, she continued to see other men, and a year after the death of their child, the Snakecharmer realized she had started seeing a new one. That's when he knew he had to kill her. Her and anyone else cheating. Before he killed her, he started spying on people at the local motels around town, checking in as Mrs. Hampton, wearing a fat suit, a dress, a wig, and sunglasses. He spotted the lying cheating bitches and planned it all out. Often the affairs began at the motels, but later they became more reckless and often started seeing each other in their homes, having sex on the sheets of their marital bed. It was always the same pattern.

The Snakecharmer was good at covering his tracks. And he would have been able to get rid of Laura's body as well, if he hadn't been interrupted by the dog. It was his own fault, though. He knew that much. He had spent too much time on his little ritual, on washing her and sitting with his head in her lap. He liked to do that to his victims, like he had done to his mother after he killed her. He had kept her in his room for days, while his father was in the hospital. He had slept with her in his bed and sat with his head in her lap, pretending she was caressing him like he had always dreamt she would. He had finally been close to his mother like he had longed for all of his childhood. Finally, she was there for him. All of his childhood, he had feared his mother would leave him. Every day he was afraid she would be gone when he came back from school. He knew that was what she wanted. He knew she didn't want to stay with him. He wasn't enough reason for her to stay. But now, he didn't have to be scared anymore.

Finally, she couldn't leave.

76

February 2015

I called Joel at the station and asked him to run the license plate. Meanwhile, Shannon and I drove up A1A, looking for the truck.

We drove across the bridge to the mainland and tried all the motels we could find to see if the truck was there. Shannon was anxious and constantly biting her nails, but another side to her had also shown itself. A determined side that wanted to find Angela and get her home. We had been so close, and Shannon was certain her daughter had to be close by.

I thought she was right.

We had pulled in at a Motel 6 when my phone rang. It was Yamilla.

"I have something I want to run by you," she said. "Something that has been bothering me since the beginning of the case of Laura Bennett's murder."

"Yes. Fire away," I said and shut off the engine. Shannon looked frantically at her phone and found the picture of Angela for the fifteenth time today.

"I was just wondering about the husband. The case file says he was drugged with Rohypnol."

"Yes, they found it in his blood. That's why he didn't see anything or hear anything."

"But, it also says he was out cold for twenty-four hours afterwards. After he was taken to the hospital," Yamilla said.

"Yes. He was still sedated," I said. I had no idea where she was going with this.

"I was just wondering about it because usually you get knocked out like half an hour after you are slipped the drug, and with the amount he had, he would be knocked out cold for twenty-four hours. It just seems a little strange, don't you think? That he was awake and able to talk when the police came, but then out for twenty-four hours afterwards."

And that was when the last piece finally came into place. "You're saying he drugged himself. He knew the police were coming, then slipped himself some Rohypnol, and half an hour later he was out. The drug in his blood would show in the tests afterwards. That was his way of getting away with murder."

"It's a theory," she said.

"And a very good one," I said.

I hung up and looked at Shannon. This new information was important, but not as important as getting Angela back.

"Shall we take a look?" I asked.

Shannon sniffled and nodded. We got out of the car and walked across the parking lot, looking at all the plates. This new information was flickering through my head. So, Brandon Bennett had killed his own wife? But why? And had he also killed Janelle? And what about Judge Martin and Melanie and her son? I thought about old Mrs. Hampton, who had stayed in room one-fifteen, when suddenly I spotted the truck in front of a room. I grabbed the handle of my gun and approached it to be sure. I double checked the numbers. It was the same.

"He's here," I said to Shannon.

She lit up. "You found it? Does that mean Angela is here as well?"

"That's what we're about to find out."

77

February 2015

Shannon could hardly contain her anxiety. Could it really be? Was Angela at the motel? Was she somewhere behind one of those many blue doors with numbers on them? Jack was speaking with the woman behind the counter. She was slightly reluctant in giving him the information, even after seeing Jack's badge and hearing how it was all part of an ongoing investigation.

Kidnapping, he called it.

"I'm not happy about this," she said, as she gave him the number of the room belonging to the owner of the truck outside. "This is a place where our guests can have their privacy."

Jack got the number, then grumbled something Shannon didn't hear before he returned to her. "Got it," he said. "Room 202."

Shannon was biting her nails. She was so scared. Jack was armed, and she watched him as his hand rested on the shaft of the gun in his belt. She'd never liked guns. Shannon had grown up on a farm, where guns were a part of life. Until her brother accidentally shot and killed himself one day. Since then, Shannon had believed guns were the worst thing man ever had created. Next to religion. Shannon loved God, but she hated religion. She never believed God meant for us to have religion. Just like he never meant for us to have guns to kill each other.

But, right now, she was glad Jack had one. There was no telling what this kidnapper was up to. Not after he tried to shoot them down in that parking lot.

Jack stopped and looked at her. "You better stay back," he said. "If this guy starts shooting again…"

"I wanna be there. I want to see my daughter," she said, pressing the tears back. She missed Angela so terribly now it was unbearable. To know that she might be this close now… she didn't want Jack to know how scared she really was. How terrified she was of losing her daughter in this motel.

"Okay. But stay behind me, all right?" Jack said with worried eyes. He too was concerned about how this was going to go down. He had wanted to involve more police and call for back up, but Shannon had begged him not to. It would only make the situation worse, if the kidnapper felt he was up against a wall. He would only harm Angela, she said.

"All I want is to get my daughter back—alive," she had told him.

She could tell by his eyes that he agreed with her. Calling for more police might escalate the situation to an extent where it got out of control. He didn't want that either. If the kidnapper felt like he still had a chance to get away, then he might be more open to negotiations. Shannon would be willing to give him more money, if he wanted. She didn't care about money. He could have everything she owned, for all she cared. She had been poor before. And she had been a whole of a lot happier then than she was now.

"The lady at the desk told me there were three kids in the room, two boys and a girl," Jack said with a low voice. "I don't know who those boys are, but I'm guessing they're not his. But this means we need to be very careful to not hurt any of the children. I will not shoot unless it is entirely necessary, do you understand? So, don't do anything unless I tell you to. All right?"

Shannon bit her lip. It was getting numb from all the biting. She nodded. She was glad he was being careful.

She held her breath as Jack clenched his fist and knocked on the door. A rather heavy woman opened the door. She was wearing a flowery dress and sunglasses. She was holding a baby in her arms. She smiled.

"Yes?"

78

February 2015

"Well, hello there, Officer Jack," the woman said.

I stared at her. She looked like Mrs. Hampton, but how could it be? I had only seen her a few times at the motel, but I was pretty sure it was her. But, who was the baby in her arms? It looked an awful lot like Sebastian Schultz...

What the heck was going on?

I was confused, but one thing I did know for certain. Something was very wrong here. My hand resting on the handle of my gun tightened its grip. I really didn't want to have to pull my gun and endanger the life of the child in her arms and whoever else was in the room behind her.

"I had a feeling you might stop by," she said. The baby in her arms burst into tears. The woman tried to comfort her. As she moved her arm, I spotted a gun underneath her dress. She pulled it out and held it to the child's head. Shannon gasped behind me.

"Lose the gun, Officer, or the kid dies."

I pulled it out and placed it on the ground. Mrs. Hampton picked it up. "Now, get in here," she said. "Hands where I can see them."

We both put our hands behind our necks and walked

inside the motel room. Mrs. Hampton closed the door behind us and locked it.

"Mommy!"

Angela ran towards Shannon and threw herself in her arms. Shannon was shaking heavily as she held her daughter in her arms. Tears were streaming across her face. Angela's hair had been colored and cut short.

"Where were you, Mommy? I couldn't find you."

"I was looking for you, sweetie. And now I found you. I'm so happy to have found you."

"Mommy, the man has a gun," she said.

I turned and looked at Mrs. Hampton. She put the baby down, then removed her sunglasses. Looking into her chilly black eyes, I immediately recognized who was hiding behind them.

It was Brandon Bennett.

"You?"

"Yes, me, Officer Jack Ryder. Thanks for all the help with my suitcases, by the way. You sure are helpful to a lady. Especially when the suitcases are as heavy as dead body weight."

I felt sick to my stomach. "You had them in the suitcases, didn't you? Your victims? You had Melanie and Sebastian Schultz in the suitcases?"

"I like my women light," he said with a grin, as the wig came off. "But, no. I would never do that to a child. Will here was always with me."

Brandon Bennett handed the baby a pacifier to make him calm. Sebastian Schultz stopped crying and sucked eagerly on the pacifier. He found a block that he started playing with. He seemed like he was well fed and had been well taken care of. I couldn't believe it.

"What's going on, Dad?" It was Ben. He came out from the restroom.

"We have visitors," Brandon Bennett said. "You remember Detective Jack Ryder, right?"

Ben nodded and sat on the bed. I wondered if he knew what his dad had been up to lately.

Brandon Bennett took off the dress and zipped down his fat suit. "Boy, it gets warm in these things," he said. "Son, could you help me a little?" Ben got up and helped his dad get out of the female body suit. Brandon made sure to still be pointing his gun at us while getting out. Underneath, he was wearing a shirt and pants. His sweat had left marks under the armpits of his light blue shirt. He picked up a fake moustache and put it on. It looked awfully real.

"I must admit," he said. "I was tempted to finish you off at the parking lot, while I had the chance. But I was hoping you would follow me here. You see, Officer, we have a lot to talk about. Now, please sit down."

He pointed the gun at two chairs he had placed in the middle of the room, back to back. Shannon and I looked at one another. There was no way around it. We had to do as he told us. For the children's sake. We sat down with our backs to each other and Brandon Bennett grabbed a roll of duct tape and started taping us to the chairs, then taping my hands in front of me, putting tape on my wrists.

"They always do this in the movies," he said, grinning.

"You watch way too much TV," I said.

"Well, that's what happens when your wife inherits millions. You don't have to work. There isn't much to do when you don't have to work, is there? Well, I could go out and have an affair like so many other men, but my wife beat me to it, didn't she? Ah, you know all about that, Officer Jack."

"I know some," I said, thinking about Tom. Had Brandon Bennett killed his wife because she slept with Tom?

"Yeah, but there is a lot you don't know."

"Like what? Tell me. Explain all this to me," I said.

"Please, sir. Please don't tie up my mother," Angela said. "Don't hurt her. She's a good mother. I promise you."

"NO!" Brandon yelled. "No, she is not a good mother!" His hand was shaking as he pointed the gun at Shannon's head.

Angela cried. "Please. Please, don't hurt her."

"She's about to ruin everything," he yelled so hard spit was flying. "She needs to understand that when you fool around you DESTROY lives. Children's lives. Husband's lives. Everything falls apart. Everything."

I was starting to see a picture. "Your mother cheated, didn't she?" I asked Brandon. "She cheated on you and your father? She hurt you. Both of you. Is that why you hurt Melanie? Is that why you hurt Laura? Because they were cheating? Did you hurt your mother as well?"

Brandon looked at me. His nostrils were flaring rapidly. He looked like a madman. It terrified me.

"I made her stay with me," he said, his voice cracking. "She hurt us, so I hurt her so she couldn't leave us. I made her stay with me. I made her love me."

"Just like you did to Laura and Melanie. You killed your mother, but it didn't satisfy your need, your desire; it didn't make the pain go away. So now, you keep killing her over and over again. Starting with Janelle, your girlfriend."

Brandon Bennett stared at me, pointing the gun at my face. His anger turned into a smile.

"I've been looking forward to having this little chat with you, Officer Jack Ryder," he said. "Or should I say, Detective? Yes, you have come far in your career, haven't you? Homicide detective. Just like your old man. Before he retired and became a motel owner."

I froze. What was this? How did he know about my dad? He had been a detective back in Ft. Lauderdale, but that was many years ago. He had retired early.

"How do you know about my father?" I asked.

"Ah, you don't know, do you? Let's just say I bumped into him once…in my apartment. What was he doing there? Oh, yes, that's right. He was doing MY MOTHER!"

79

February 2015

I couldn't believe my own ears. Was he really saying what I thought he was? My dad? My father? Albert Ryder? Cheating on his wife of forty years? No. It couldn't be. I was shocked. My mother and father were so into each other. They loved each other; they would never…he would never.

"Yeah, that's right," Brandon Bennett continued. "Your beloved father slept with my mother and destroyed my entire existence. Why do you think I chose his motel? Why do you think you're sitting here?"

"So, you're doing this to me because of my dad?" I asked. "You want to kill me?"

Brandon Bennett laughed loudly. "Oh, I have something better in mind. You see, I have already done something to you."

My heart dropped. I thought about the children. Abigail, Austin, Emily. Had he hurt them somehow? Then, I thought about my parents. Had he hurt my parents? The blood was rushing through my veins. My anger was rising at the very thought of him being close to anyone in my family.

Brandon Bennett reached into his pocket and pulled out something. He held it between his fingers in front of my face. My heart stopped.

It was a ring. A very special ring.

"How did you get that?" I asked, trying to get out of the chair.

"I took it off her finger," he said, holding it up in the light. "As a souvenir. After I killed her back in 2012."

I went completely numb. Every cell in my body screamed in pain. "You killed her? You killed Arianna?"

Brandon Bennett's eyes shone when he looked at me. "Yes. Isn't it beautiful? Your dad destroyed my family, and now I have destroyed his. You and your kids have been miserable without her. And now you know why she never came back. She was on her way, though. I found her in North Carolina. She wanted to come back to you; she told her friend at the diner where she had worked for a couple of months while figuring her life out. She told her friend she was going back to Cocoa Beach the following week to be with her husband and children…that she had been thinking it through and realized what she had. That she loved you and the kids, but just needed some time. Isn't it perfect? I grabbed her in her studio, sedated her, and took her to the motel. To your father's motel. I kept her there for a week before I strangled her in the bath-tub. I sedated her, then when she woke up, I let her watch her children come and go from the window. The desperation on her face was priceless. She whimpered when she could hear their little voices. Oh, how badly she wanted to be with them again. I sedated her with chloroform and washed her every night. Washed her with bleach to clean the impurity from the other man she had slept with. I even sang to her. You want to know what I sang?"

I couldn't even answer. I wanted to scream; I wanted to yell, but I couldn't. I was too stunned, too torn apart in pain and sorrow. I could hardly breathe.

"You really can't guess it? I sang Hit the Road, Jack, of course," he said, and laughed. "No, seriously. I did you a favor there. She was sleeping around. Would have made you so miserable if she had ever come back to you. Once a cheater always a cheater."

If I hadn't been tied down, I would have killed him on the spot. The cruelty of what he had done felt like a kick in the stomach. I had no more words. Shannon was crying next to me.

"You sick bastard," she yelled at him.

Brandon Bennett walked to her and knelt in front of her. He stroked her cheek. I could sense how she shivered in terror and anger.

"I know Joe didn't treat you right," he said. "But that's not an excuse for sleeping around like some WHORE!"

Shannon jumped when he yelled at her. Angela cried. I tried to gather my thoughts. I kept picturing Arianna. It hurt so badly inside of me, knowing she had been so close, knowing I could have saved her, had I only known she was right there, right in that room where I walked past every day when picking up the children from the school bus. Arianna hadn't left me and stayed away. She had wanted to come back. She had been planning on it. Oh, the terror of knowing this. I didn't know if I would ever be able to live with that knowledge.

"Now," Brandon Bennett said, and looked at us. "I have to figure out what to do with the two of you. The kids and I have to go, you see. We're flying out tonight from Ft. Lauderdale to Grand Cayman, where all this nice money is waiting for us, and where no one can reach us. We might stay there, we might continue to another island, who knows? At least the kids will be safe from their parents and all their crap. But first, I have to get rid of her," he said, and pointed the gun at Shannon. "Jack, I'll let you live. I need you to remember what I did to you for every day for the rest of your life. I need you to tell your father what he did and what I did in return. Otherwise, it will all be in vain, right?"

I had stopped looking at him. Instead, my eyes had locked with those of Ben. Something had stirred inside of him. I looked at my gun on the dresser, where Brandon had put it, then back at Ben, who now saw it too.

80

February 2015

"I T ENDS HERE, DAD."

The gun in Ben's hands was shaking heavily. So was his voice when he spoke.

Brandon Bennett turned around and looked at his son, who was pointing the gun at him. My gun. I had no idea if the kid had ever held one in his hands before, let alone fired one. Would he be able to fire at his dad if he had to? I wasn't so sure. He was, after all, just five years old.

"Ben? What the...? What are you doing, buddy? We're a team, remember? You and me?"

Ben shook his head. He was sweating heavily. "Not any more, Dad. You killed Mom. I can't let this go on anymore. It's not right, Dad. What we're doing is not right."

Brandon Bennett was getting angry now. He took a couple of steps towards his son. Ben walked backwards.

"I will shoot you," Ben said.

Brandon Bennett stopped when he saw the seriousness in his son's eyes. "Give me the gun," he said. "Hand it over. Ben, you listen to me, Son. I don't want to hurt you. Not again, Son."

Ben started crying now. I could tell he was about to cave. He couldn't stand up to his father. At least, I thought he couldn't, but a new strength suddenly showed in him. He was crying, but also snorting in anger.

"You killed Mom," he said. "You told me you were asleep. You told me you didn't see who did it. You lied to me, Dad. You killed her. I just heard you say you did. And other women. You killed them too. They were somebody's mom, Dad. I don't care what Mom did to you. She's still my mom."

"Don't make me shoot you, Ben," Brandon Bennett yelled. "I will if I have to, Son."

The two of them were pointing their guns at each other. This was a bad situation. I feared it would end very badly.

Meanwhile, I had made eye contact with Angela and signaled her to come closer. To get out of the shooting range, in case shots were fired. She walked silently behind Brandon Bennett without him noticing it and hid behind a recliner. I put my hands high above my head and came down past my hips, causing the duct tape to split and my hands to get free.

"You always were an ungrateful kid. A real mommy's boy, huh? Well, I can get by without you."

This was going in the wrong direction.

I reached down and grabbed the duct tape on my feet and ripped it off, then sprang for Brandon's back, just as he fired a shot towards Ben.

Shannon screamed and so did Angela, while Sebastian cried from his play area on the floor. I landed on top of Brandon Bennett. The fall made the gun fly out of his hand. I threw in a couple of punches to his face and knocked him out immediately. Being an amateur boxer in my teen-years, I knew exactly how to do that to make sure he wouldn't get up anytime soon. Then I rushed towards Ben, who was on the floor in a pool of blood. Angela helped her mother get loose. Ben's small body was pulsing and he was shivering with cold already. I took off my T-shirt and tried to stop the blood with it, then screamed for Shannon to call 911.

"Don't leave us, Ben," I cried. "Stay here. Stay with us."

Epilogue
MARCH 2015

I t was a beautiful funeral ceremony at Club Zion, our local church, where Ben used to come with his mother. We were singing hymns. Shannon stood by my side, along with all of our kids and my parents. I couldn't believe all that had happened in the past couple of months. I still hadn't recuperated from what Brandon Bennett had told me about my father and Arianna. I hadn't asked my mother about any of it, whether she knew my dad had cheated or not. I decided to let it go. It was, after all, none of my business. They seemed to be doing well now and loved each other dearly. That was all I needed to know. I had decided to leave it all behind me and move on. Even Arianna.

Pastor Daniel took the stage.

"We're gathered here today to say goodbye to Ben…" The pastor paused. All eyes were on him.

"…'s right arm."

I looked at Ben, who was standing in front of the church with his dog on one side and his grandfather in a wheelchair on the other. He had lost his arm, where his dad had shot him. The boy had been depressed for days afterwards while lying in the hospital, even when his grandfather had brought him the dog. Nothing seemed to cheer him up. So, I had come up with the idea of performing a ceremony for his arm in the church, a funeral, where he could say goodbye to it. I got the idea from one of my favorite movies, Fried Green Tomatoes.

Ben had loved it, and luckily, my good friend and surf buddy, Pastor Daniel, liked the idea as well. I was happy to soothe things a little for the poor kid. He was about to leave town to go live with his aunt, the oldest of John Platt's children. She had told us she would take care of him, even though she hadn't known Laura at all.

"Family sticks together no matter what, right?" she had said when we contacted her, telling her Ben had no one else.

I felt reassured she would take good care of him. She had a husband and another kid of her own. She would provide a real family for Ben. And he needed a stable home more than anyone right now.

Brandon Bennett had been taken to a secure prison, while awaiting his trial. I was building a case against him that, hopefully, would end up keeping him in there for the rest of his life. I had, little by little, found out what he had been up to. How he had done it. He had stolen an Animal Control van many years ago, down in Ft. Lauderdale. We found the report from when it was reported stolen. He had used it to spy on the women he planned on attacking. We had found snakes at his father's house, and my theory was that he had used them to get access to these women's houses. He had simply let the snakes into their garages, and then appeared on their doorsteps and told them he was from Animal Control. No one suspected a van from Animal Control when parked in a driveway or on the street. I still didn't know exactly how many women he had killed, but he had taken pictures of his victims with his phone, and that told an entire story of its own.

My first thought was I hoped that he would get the death penalty, but now I hoped he would just suffer for the rest of his life, knowing what he had done. It was a much worse fate than death. Besides, the death penalty was very rarely used in Florida.

Sebastian Schultz had been reunited with his father and so

far they stayed with his parents till the insurance came through. He hadn't suffered any abuse or neglect while he was kidnapped according to the doctors. I hoped the boy was too young to remember what had happened to him when he grew older.

To my joy, Shannon had decided to stay in Cocoa Beach for a little longer. To get back on her feet, as she explained to the press, who soon got to hear about the entire kidnapping story and plastered it all over the newspapers and magazines. It was harder for her to avoid the spotlight now, but they still didn't know about her hideout in my apartment, where we were all staying, since my parents' motel wasn't done being examined. So far, we weren't getting on each other's nerves. I actually enjoyed having all of them close to me immensely. Especially after what had happened. Family was my top priority. And Shannon and Angela had quickly become a part of ours. Joe wasn't too happy when she told him she wasn't coming back to Nashville anytime soon, and they were facing a custody battle. It wasn't over yet. Far from it. But, we decided not to worry about it. Now was the time to heal our wounds.

I hadn't told the twins or Emily that Arianna had died yet. I would get to that eventually, and I was waiting for the right moment. First, I needed to come to terms with it myself. Yamilla had already identified the few bone-parts of the other body found at the motel as belonging to Arianna. A DNA-test confirmed it. So, it was official now. I was a widower.

"I have a surprise for you," Shannon said, when we came back to the apartment after the ceremony. She told me to close my eyes while she led me by the hand into the living room.

"Open your eyes," she said.

My eyes landed on the most beautiful orange and black 7.0 foot fun-shaped board I had ever seen in my life.

"What's this?" I asked.

"It's for me," she said. "I found a local shaper to make it for me."

"For you?"

"Yeah. I thought you could teach me how to surf while I'm here."

I laughed and kissed her. The twins made yuck-sounds behind us. They loved Shannon, and liked having her and Angela around, but didn't like it when we kissed publicly. They would have to get used to it.

"On one condition," I said.

"And what's that?"

"You teach me how to play the guitar."

Shannon smiled, then reached out her hand.

"That's a deal, Detective."

THE END

Afterword

DEAR READER,

Thank you for purchasing *Hit the Road, Jack* (JACK RYDER #1).
I have enjoyed writing this novel so much. It was great for me
to have a change of scenery, and I have already fallen deeply
in love with Jack and his family. I hope you have too, since
this is just the beginning of his journey. I will be writing the
next chapter in his life right away. Until then, check out all of
my other books by following the links below, and don't forget
to leave reviews if possible.

Take care,
  Willow

About the Author

Willow Rose is a multi-million-copy best-selling Author and an Amazon ALL-star Author of more than 60 novels. Her books are sold all over the world.

She writes Mystery, Thriller, Paranormal, Romance, Suspense, Horror, Supernatural thrillers, and Fantasy.

Willow's books are fast-paced, nail-biting pageturners with twists you won't see coming. That's why her fans call her The Queen of Scream.

Several of her books have reached the Kindle top 10 of ALL books in the US, UK, and Canada. She has sold more than three million books all over the world.

Willow lives on Florida's Space Coast with her husband and two daughters. When she is not writing or reading, you will find her surfing and watch the dolphins play in the waves of the Atlantic Ocean.

To be the first to hear about new releases and bargains from Willow Rose. Sign up to be on the VIP list below.

I promise not to share your email with anyone else, and I won't clutter your inbox.

http://readerlinks.com/1/415254

Tired of too many emails? Text the word: "willowrose" to 31996 to sign up to Willow's VIP text List to get a text alert with news about New Releases, Giveaways, Bargains and Free books from Willow.

FOLLOW WILLOW ROSE ON BOOKBUB:
https://www.bookbub.com/authors/willow-rose

Connect with Willow online:
https://www.facebook.com/willowredrose
www.willow-rose.net
http://www.goodreads.com/author/show/4804769.Willow_Rose
https://twitter.com/madamwillowrose
madamewillowrose@gmail.com

 facebook.com/willowredrose

twitter.com/madamwillowrose

instagram.com/madamewillowrose

Books by the Author

MYSTERY/THRILLER/HORROR NOVELS

- IN ONE FELL SWOOP
- UMBRELLA MAN
- BLACKBIRD FLY
- TO HELL IN A HANDBASKET
- EDWINA
- IN COLD BLOOD

7TH STREET CREW SERIES

- WHAT HURTS THE MOST
- YOU CAN RUN
- YOU CAN'T HIDE
- CAREFUL LITTLE EYES

EMMA FROST SERIES

- ITSY BITSY SPIDER
- MISS DOLLY HAD A DOLLY
- RUN, RUN AS FAST AS YOU CAN
- CROSS YOUR HEART AND HOPE TO DIE
- PEEK-A-BOO I SEE YOU
- TWEEDLEDUM AND TWEEDLEDEE
- EASY AS ONE, TWO, THREE
- THERE'S NO PLACE LIKE HOME
- SLENDERMAN
- WHERE THE WILD ROSES GROW

- WALTZING MATHILDA
- DRIP DROP

JACK RYDER SERIES

- HIT THE ROAD JACK
- SLIP OUT THE BACK JACK
- THE HOUSE THAT JACK BUILT
- BLACK JACK
- GIRL NEXT DOOR
- HER FINAL WORD

REBEKKA FRANCK SERIES

- ONE, TWO...HE IS COMING FOR YOU
- THREE, FOUR...BETTER LOCK YOUR DOOR
- FIVE, SIX...GRAB YOUR CRUCIFIX
- SEVEN, EIGHT...GONNA STAY UP LATE
- NINE, TEN...NEVER SLEEP AGAIN
- ELEVEN, TWELVE...DIG AND DELVE
- THIRTEEN, FOURTEEN...LITTLE BOY UNSEEN
- BETTER NOT CRY
- TEN LITTLE GIRLS
- IT ENDS HERE

HORROR SHORT-STORIES

- MOMMY DEAREST
- THE BIRD
- BETTER WATCH OUT
- EENIE, MEENIE
- ROCK-A-BYE BABY
- NIBBLE, NIBBLE, CRUNCH
- HUMPTY DUMPTY

- CHAIN LETTER

SCIENCE FICTION/PARANORMAL ROMANCE/FANTASY NOVELS

- THE SURGE
- GIRL DIVIDED

THE VAMPIRES OF SHADOW HILLS

- FLESH AND BLOOD
- BLOOD AND FIRE
- FIRE AND BEAUTY
- BEAUTY AND BEASTS
- BEASTS AND MAGIC
- MAGIC AND WITCHCRAFT
- WITCHCRAFT AND WAR
- WAR AND ORDER
- ORDER AND CHAOS
- CHAOS AND COURAGE

AFTERLIFE SERIES

- BEYOND
- SERENITY
- ENDURANCE
- COURAGEOUS

THE WOLFBOY CHRONICLES

- A GYPSY SONG
- I AM WOLF

DAUGHTERS OF THE JAGUAR

- SAVAGE
- BROKEN